## Praise for
## A TERRIBLE LOVE

# A TERRIBLE LOVE

## MARATA EROS

**G**

GALLERY BOOKS

NEW YORK   LONDON   TORONTO   SYDNEY   NEW DELHI

# G

Gallery Books
A Division of Simon & Schuster, Inc.
1230 Avenue of the Americas
New York, NY 10020

First Gallery Books trade paperback edition September 2013

GALLERY BOOKS and colophon are registered trademarks of Simon & Schuster, Inc.

For information about special discounts for bulk purchases, please contact Simon & Schuster Special Sales at 1-866-506-1949 or business@simonandschuster.com.

The Simon & Schuster Speakers Bureau can bring authors to your live event. For more information or to book an event contact the Simon & Schuster Speakers Bureau at 1-866-248-3049 or visit our website at www.simonspeakers.com.

Interior design by Akasha Archer

Manufactured in the United States of America

10 9 8 7 6 5 4 3 2 1

Library of Congress Cataloging-in-Publication Data is available.

ISBN 978-1-4767-5219-8
ISBN 978-1-4767-5159-7 (ebook)

*My steadfast husband,*
*you helped me be who I was meant to be.*
*I love you.*

*You're Mine*
by Tragedy Machine

*No point trying to deny*
*you're my prisoner for the taking*
*you're mine . . .*
*you're my perfect glass for the breaking*
*you're mine . . .*

# PROLOGUE

The solid wooden doors of the closet shake as he pounds them. "I'll hurt her, Jewell," he says in a voice thickened by his usual rage. Thwack, punch, rattle. "And there's not a fucking thing you can do about it!"

I clench my eyes, arms wrapped around my knees; if I ignore him he'll go away. He always used to.

But it's different this time. Faith came. She knew something was wrong and she came.

I listen to her wail in the background, sweat beading on the tender part of my upper lip as I roll it in my mouth to keep from crying out. I thought I could hide.

I thought it would end if I ignored it.

I kept the secret, but now, as my stepbrother assaults the only friend I've ever had, I squeeze my head between my knees and shake with my silent sobbing.

It's me he wants to hurt. It's me he'll punish in this horrible moment of suspended time; Faith is merely the vehicle.

Faith is in the wrong place at exactly the wrong time.

Her arguing got Thaddeus to notice her. However, Faith will never submit.

Her pleas go unheeded. I bear witness in a dark locked closet; shamed, terrified and soaking in my own sweat and tears, I hear what he does and I can't stop it.

Faith saved me, and my apathy is murdering her.

## Black

Black is everywhere; it's in the sky, the ground, the pounding rain that pings off the casket.

It's on my dress.

My shoes. The umbrellas are a sea of it, rolling endlessly on and on.

But there is one spot that's red. The flare of my mother's dress I can see from just beyond the polished lip of the wood.

My stepbrother meets my eyes with the deep gray of his own and I shudder with keen revulsion.

I count backward silently, the tears that scald my face chilling as the rain meets them, mingling with them in a dance of sadness that washes my face. Though it doesn't cleanse the guilt. It never will.

He gives me a little smirk and I cast my eyes down so he can't see the burning hatred in my gaze.

Thad thinks he's home free. His crime buried beneath the prestige of his standing in the community.

He hasn't counted on how far I'll go to secure his future destruction. And my own survival. I'd do it all.

For Faith.

I suck in a shuddering breath, my plan firmly in place, my fear as well.

I drop a single deep-cream rose on Faith's casket. It spins in slow motion, making a soft thump as it connects with the mirrored finish, and I turn to leave, the good-bye caught in my heart for eternity.

The reporters are already here.

I flee, my high heels stabbing the sodden earth beneath my feet. When the limousine driver opens the door for me I slide inside, breathing a sigh of relief when I see I share it with no one. My vacant mother and stepfather will dutifully stay and shore up my best friend's parents against the tragic loss of their daughter. For duty's sake, not empathy's.

Thaddeus MacLeod stands watching my limo, the closing glass of my window beginning to shield me from him. As the reporters gather around him he has eyes only for me. I shiver at that quiet look of contained menace, despairing. I gather my resolve like fragile collected blossoms.

*I can do this.*

"Thaddeus!" I hear a woman reporter yell. "What does Senator MacLeod think of your attempted rescue of your dear family friend?" She heaves a microphone above her head and toward Thad's face, skimming the heads of reporters who stand in front of her.

He turns his face away from mine and even in the dim light of the outside I can see his one-hundred-watt smile come online, dazzling the reporter who posed the question. It makes me want to hurl. There's no food in my stomach but my body goes through the motions nonetheless.

I let the glass swallow the view, turning away and sinking into the plush leather as I allow my tears to come.

Our limo driver flicks his eyes to my wet face in the rear-view mirror, then discreetly away.

I hit the *up* button on the divider and the glass partition slides up.

It is the last moment of grief I'll allow myself. Soon I will run.

Toward anonymity, freedom. And maybe someday, absolution.

# ONE

~

*Two years later*

"Jess!" Carlie calls, chasing after me. I listen to the rat-tat-tat of her high-heeled boots stabbing the poor hallway behind me.

God, if it is another scheme to get me to go along with some crazy-ass plan . . . I'm going to be pissed.

"Jess!" she shouts, and I turn.

It's impossible to stay mad at Carlie; she is too over-the-top ridiculous for words. My eyes take in her customary look, the perfectly coiffed hair, the skinny jeans jammed into second-skin boots that somehow house thinly knit leg warmers. And don't even get me started on what she rams her boobs into. It is surely a manacle for tits.

How did she get them to look like that? I shake my head and smile despite myself.

"She smiles! Excellent!" Carlie runs and throws her arms around me, saying in an uncharacteristic whisper, "Look what

I have, girlfriend." She waves a paper around in my face like a flag.

I can't make anything out, it's just a grayish blur. "Stop that, ya tool!" I say with false rage.

Carlie gives me the bird and holds it steady in front of my face. The words come together in a collision of—*no*. "I'm not going," I say, beginning to walk away.

"You are *so* going," Carlie says. Then softly she calls, "Jess."

I stand with my back to her as other students ram through the hall, jostling and loud, maybe a minute left until class.

"What?" I ask, still not turning.

"It's *ballet*," she says.

"I know," I whisper. I break out in a light sweat, an automatic response. The opportunity to indulge my passion for dance, my former privileged life's only oasis, now teases me with its nearness.

"They're coming here . . . to our school. You could, like . . . audition."

*I could.* "No, Carlie."

She takes me at my word, throwing the paper in the trash and slinging an arm around my neck. Carlie uses me for balance as she totters around on her stilettos. "You have to admit it was a good idea."

I look up into her face; she's a damn Amazonian. "Yeah," I say.

"You can't run forever, Jess."

Her words jolt me, but then I realize Carlie is just using an expression. She isn't being literal.

It seems a little too easy; she's usually a dog with a bone.

Carlie stops hanging off me like a monkey and we part ways for our respective courses.

I listen to the sound of her heels as they echo down the nearly empty hall.

I take a deep breath and pass through the door for English lit class. Just one of many sophomores in a generic university in the great state of Washington. I like blending in.

My life depends on it.

～

Ballet was my life—before. I can't give it up, because it won't give me up. The music plays in my head night and day. It's a wonder I ever get anything accomplished. Some of the other students might see a subtle bob of my head and wonder. I smile at the looks and stare off into space during lectures.

I do a similar internal music routine when I work at the coffee shop like a good drone; my partial scholarship at the University of Washington requires a little sideline income. I'm lucky to have it. I had to test out of a bunch of freshman courses, prove proficiency and then cop out as poor. I certainly couldn't use my former grades and prestigious private school to get the full ride I'd had. That was from *before*.

It was all worth it. The stress, the work.

Then Carlie wormed her way inside my defenses despite every obstacle I'd thrown up in her way. Declared herself my friend when it went against every promise I'd made to myself. I broke them all with our friendship. What she sees in me I'll never know.

Carlie knows about the ballet barre I installed in my dorm room, which doesn't have space for it; it's pretty tough to hide and it's my only décor. A huge metal bar driven into studs behind drywall. Yeah, so beautiful. I move my bed every day and go to sleep each night looking at it. Trying to forget. Ballet blanks the pain; it's the eraser of my memories.

Each day I execute my barre exercises, just as I did every day when I was another girl. Now I am a woman, with woman-sized desires and dreams. My traumatic memories haven't robbed me of my humanity. No matter what happens there's a stubborn spark that wants to live.

Carlie has begun something inside me with the whisper of the ballet company visiting the U Dub campus. I ignore that something, beat at it when it appears, reject it, but it refuses to let go and blooms inside me.

Hope.

It's all Carlie's fault. I was just fine when I didn't have any.

Now it's here and there is no hiding from it.

I open my mouth as I put the blue contact in, blinking once, hoping the damn thing will sit correctly. I'll never take having perfect vision my whole life for granted again. At the end of the day I can't wait to tear the suckers out of my eyes; they dry up like popcorn farts and burn like hell.

I stand away from the mirror, applying the barest hint of colored lip gloss, giving my eyeballs time to rest from the abuse of inserting contacts. I brush my teeth, squirt vanilla body spray on all the high points and cover my deep-ginger lashes with chocolate-colored mascara.

I flutter them and decide they look just right. Next, I plait my hair into two thick braids. Even braided my hair is past my breasts; its former deep auburn is now dark blond. Its length is my only concession to my former life. Despite its length, it is nondescript, nearly invisible.

Just like I want it.

I study my hairline for roots. Finding none, I step away from the mirror, then turn back to it and stick my tongue out.

It's a glaring blue from the Blow Pop I've just ruthlessly sucked on.

I need to grow up.

I saunter off just as the knock comes at my door.

Carlie doesn't wait for an invitation, she just bursts in.

I put my hands on my hips. "Why bother knocking?" I laugh.

She flicks her hair over a shoulder and puckers her lips, giving a dismissive shrug.

I don't see her stuff my ballet slippers in her backpack.

"Ready?" she asks innocently.

"Yeah, just . . ." I collect a few things, ramming them into my oversized Guess purse, which I swing over my shoulder.

It's a rare day off and I am really dragging ass. I'm sore from the barre and twirling in the middle of a dorm room with only the walls watching my perfect performance.

Pathetic.

"You wore makeup," Carlie says, eyeballing my pathetic attempt to look cute.

"Does mascara and lip gloss qualify?" I ask.

"Hell, yeah! Especially for you," she exclaims vigorously. "Miss au naturel." She giggles behind her hand.

"Bitch," I say.

"Sticks and stones and all that happy ho-ho shit," she replies, completely unperturbed by my shameless name-calling.

"Why did you tell me to wear makeup?" I ask, suspicious as I cross my arms underneath my breasts, my eyes narrowing. I slam my dorm door, rattling the knob to ensure it's locked. It never closes right.

We move away from the door and I impatiently wait for her response.

Carlie's brows arch and she pouts at me. "Because: you *will* look attractive to the opposite sex. If it takes my last breath, you will look cute even while we sweat."

I look down at my yoga pants, the turned band at the top a muted tie-dye pattern, with a tight deep-blue tee and my braided hair rounding out the hippie-chic thing I've got going on.

"I think you'll have to try harder," I say.

"If you were just sluttier," Carlie says mournfully, hiding behind her dark curly hair.

I slug her and she yelps, giving me hurt eyes, then she smiles. "I'll wear ya down, you'll see."

"Never!" I stab the air with my fist as we turn the corner and a wall of noise hits me. Everywhere I look there are students, older adults and an odd assortment of people I've never seen. It's too much to take in. I turn to Carlie; obviously, we totally can't work out today.

"Hey," I say, looking into the deep auditorium that doubles as a gym. "What's going on . . . what are all these people doing?"

But Carlie's already moving and doesn't hear my question.

An older woman is seated behind a folding desk and Carlie speeds to the desk, her flats making no sound as they whisper across the floor.

She signs in to some ledger and I start taking it in.

A totally hot guy comes to me with a numbered paper and a safety pin. "Hey," he says, and I stare numbly at him. I can't think of a thing to say.

"Hi!" Carlie blurts from beside me, fluttering her sooty eyelashes at La Hunk. "This is my friend Jess Mackey."

Hunk smiles at me and I sink into his pale gray eyes—drown, more like. "I'm Mitch," he says.

I stare.

Carlie elbows me with a traitorous cackle. *God, can she be more obvious?* "I'm Jess," I stick out my hand and he swallows it in his own.

"I know." He smirks and a dimple flashes into place, disappearing just as quickly. He swings back long dark hair that refuses to stay out of his eyes.

"Right," I say, heat flooding my face.

He steps into my private bubble and my flush deepens; my heart starts to speed when he reaches for my thin T-shirt and I shrink away from him.

"It's okay," he murmurs beside my face, his minty breath tickling the sensitive skin there. "I'm attaching your number."

*What number?*

I look around and see about fifty girls with their hair slicked back in tight buns, some high, some on the nape because they've been zapped with the unlucky thick-hair gene like yours truly.

Realization slams into me.

The Seattle Pacific Ballet Company has arrived. This is the audition Carlie tried to bully me into attending a few days ago. Heat suffuses my body in a sickening nauseous wave. I turn to leave and Mitch puts a staying hand gently on my arm. He jerks his jaw toward where a mock stage has been set up. "It's this way, dancing girl." He smiles, his teeth very white in his face.

"I can't do it . . . I'm not signed up," I say, folding my arms again, the paper with my audition number crinkling underneath the gesture.

His smile widens into a grin as he dips his head to look at a clipboard that just magically appears. Mitch runs a long, tapered finger down the assembled names until he reaches midway. He taps it once and I jump slightly. He lifts his chin, a light dusting of dark stubble sprinkled on the slight cleft that bisects it. "There you are," he says softly. "Mackey, Jess."

He sweeps his hand in front of me; I give a death glare to Carlie and my traitor friend winks at me.

I can't *not* audition without looking like an ass.

My feet are dragging like lead fills my shoes.

*My slippers!*

Carlie jogs to my side and hands me my ballet slippers. I seethe at her; she smiles sweetly and whispers, "Break a leg."

I gaze at the stage like it's the fabled pirate's plank. My

stomach clenches as I move to take my place in line and watch the girl onstage.

She's perfect . . . breathtaking.

The music ends softly and she moves off the stage. The judges whisper and I know immediately who they'll choose.

It won't be me.

I think of Faith and what she would have wanted. I think of how I love her still. Of how this dream of Faith's that I reach my full potential, that I escape the madness of a household ruled by indifferent tyranny and jealousy born of privilege and entitlement come to an end . . . and a new beginning. Thad can't reach me here, and this is my way to honor Faith and, in so doing, myself.

Then an extraordinary thing happens. When it is my turn I float up the steps and onto the temporary stage as they put on *Moonlight Sonata* by Beethoven.

It's from before.

The notes breathe through the auditorium, making the fine hairs of my neck stand at attention. The music robs me of thought, forcing my body to execute moves I forgot I knew. My arms sweep, and I pirouette, spinning and snapping my head to find my corner. The soreness from earlier melts away as my body heats with familiarity. As I whip my leg up, my foot is parallel to my head for a fraction of time and then I land softly, only to immediately rise to the balls of my feet as I approach the judges with their riveted stares. The length of the song and its sad ending beg my limbs to undulate in a perfectly timed flutter of classic swan arms. I draw nearer still while keeping my elbows level as my arms float in a wavelike pattern and the balls of my feet propel me forward just as the final piano notes fall.

Then once more their sorrowful notes swell and fill the auditorium in melancholy triumph.

I stop, dipping into a graceful plié, and assume first position.

My hands are cupped slightly and I tilt my head, looking off to the right of my position.

The utter lack of noise causes me to look at the judges as I relax my shoulders and my hands drop gracefully to my sides.

They have stood and every eye is on me. Including the gray gaze of a certain hunk named Mitch.

When the applause breaks out I don't know whether to cry or run.

In the end, I stay.

My eyes scan the crowd and notice the one person who does not clap.

A man leans against the back of the cavernous gym auditorium, his black eyes seeming to attack me, and I take an involuntary step backward from the burning intensity of his gaze.

Carlie interrupts the moment, throwing herself at me.

"I knew you could," she whispers, strangling me in an epic hug that cuts off my airway.

I gently push her away and look for that disconcerting male presence. Hostile.

But he is gone.

Just like he was never there.

# TWO

⁓

I'm staring off into space again, my pencil stuck into the knot of my messy bun, as the lecture about genetics drones on. Too bad I haven't been able get out of biology. I would love to miss it.

No such luck.

I haven't been worth anything since the surprise audition. I'm still kinda pissed at Carlie, not that it helps. She's convinced that my extracurricular activities are the key to my coming out of my shell. I sigh, doodling again. My scribbling noises are lost in the cavernous, theater-style classroom, built to hold three hundred students. I always sit in the same seat, the most unidentifiable: upper left side . . . no man's land.

I look up when the same guy who always sits by me heaves himself into the seat, three minutes late to class, and tosses his legs underneath the seat in front of him, bumping the person's backpack out from underneath the chair. "Nice," I whisper.

"Damn straight," he says, then his hooded eyes take in the disgruntled glance that comes his way and he flips off the captain-of-the-team type in front of him.

"Had a weekend, I see," I say, and he winks, looking pretty rough.

"Yeah, busted out a party that took no prisoners. It was tight."

As I look at Brad I wish I had his easy way. He just floats through life, no cares, parties on the weekend, plays guitar with some band when he can get a gig and plows through biology effortlessly.

I have to work to get a decent grade in the sciences. They were always a weak spot.

I sigh again.

"All tied up knitting this weekend?" Brad asks with a smirk, giving me a sidelong look.

I shift in my seat, squelching an interior flutter. "Actually, I auditioned for the Seattle Pacific Ballet." I don't mention that my friend shoved me through the door, a hot guy dazed me with his natural charm and they happened to play a song I already had a routine for burned into my brain since . . . forever.

"Really," Brad drawls, playing with a rubber band that snaps annoyingly as he twists it into shapes too complicated to follow.

"Yeah," I answer softly.

"Well"—he looks at me with his deep chocolate eyes—"I bet you kicked everyone's ass, Jess."

I shake my head in the negative and the jock in front of Brad turns around and says, "Some of us are trying to learn here, Gunner."

I raise my eyebrows, surprised the guy in front of us knows Brad's last name. Hell, I didn't.

"Yeah?" Brad asks, his eyebrows shooting to his hairline. "Fuck off, Brock."

The guy whose name is apparently Brock begins to rise and our biology professor's glance shifts away from his lecture-podium notes. "Is there a problem, gentlemen?"

Brock and Brad square off and I'm surprised to notice the jock doesn't look that much bigger than Brad.

Brad says nothing, just stares. "No problem, Professor Steuben," Brock says, finally relenting. He settles back into his seat but gives me a glare before he faces forward. Brad frowns at his notice of me.

*Guilty by association,* I think. I slink down into my chair and hope that I can remain unnoticeable for the rest of the semester. God, it's only what? October?

Brad throws himself in his seat again and blasts his biker boots back underneath the jock's seat.

I can't help it, a small giggle escapes me, and Brock turns around and glares at me. My smile fades and Brad pats my arm, a funny gesture from a six-foot-two guy in all leather, with tattoos and shit-kickers as staples of his look.

"Don't worry, he's a pussy." Brad shrugs and turns to face forward, actually giving his attention to the lecture.

I keep a straight face somehow and nod. "Yeah, no worries here." I giggle. And I see Brock tense.

He knows we're laughing at him but I can't seem to help myself.

Brad walks me out of class and turns as we're leaving to say, "You need some help with this?" He points at the latest home-work packet. It's so thick it's practically a novel.

I look helplessly at the Punnett square booklet I'll have to decipher later. I took this crap in high school but don't remem-ber all the details of eye color and predictions of stuff any better now. It's a formula and I'm sort of a dreamer. Yeah, kind of a bad mix.

Brad gives me a smile full of snark, his dark eyes roaming my face for a second, then he says, "Here," and before I can say no he grabs my cell and inputs his number. "Text me if you need help with this crap," he says. "I got your back, dancer."

"You already knew!" I semi-wail when he winks.

"Who doesn't?" he says innocently, then does the shittiest pirouette I've ever seen as I laugh at how ridiculous this big guy looks attempting ballet. Brad tugs on the topknot of my hair, swings his black mop behind his shoulder and smolders off, all black leather and attitude. He looks menacing but he doesn't fool me; Brad's a marshmallow on the inside.

I look after him for a moment, then stumble forward when a backpack makes hard contact between my shoulder blades. I look around for who nailed me and it's Brock the Jock.

"Watch it, girlie," he says slowly, and smiles.

The smile doesn't reach his eyes.

I swallow hard and then another pair of eyes catches mine.

Gray eyes like pale storm clouds.

I glance back at Brock and he gives me a hard look and

then is lost in the sea of students. It seems like I've been put on notice.

I try to shake it off, but my uneasiness is slow to leave me.

Mitch approaches me and I have the same jar of captured butterflies in my stomach I had when he pinned that number on my shirt.

I still have the paper with the number.

"Hey," he says, and I notice that sexy stubble remains on his chin as I try to wake myself up from my shyness.

Mitch looks after the disappearing Brock and asks, "You know him?"

I shake my head.

"That was a pretty hard blow," he says, his gaze darkening at the empty spot in the hall where Brock just was.

*Is that worry in his voice?* I wonder.

"No, I don't know him . . . he sits in front of me in biology." I can't help but say the class name with disdain and he laughs softly, his voice a deep vibration that feels like it moves through my chest in a purr.

I laugh and we stand awkwardly for a few moments. "Ah," I say, "I need to go, physics is way across campus . . ."

"Oh wow, okay . . . you're a . . ."

"Sophomore," I respond neutrally, my body starting to tense like it always does beyond question one. That's why I get along with Brad so well: he doesn't ask personal questions.

"You're a masochist then?" he asks.

I pause, a tingling beginning to creep up on my skin. "What?" I ask, sort of horrified but mildly titillated by the unexpected word.

"Y'know, biology, then physics . . . in a row." He smiles and I know he's joking. He almost had me there.

Then I see him, like a dark shadow out of the corner of my eye as he stalks toward us. I can't believe I ever thought Brad's eyes were brown when I see this guy's.

Or that Brad smoldered at all.

This guy makes Brad look like an ember, a banked fire compared to a roaring inferno.

I stand there burning up as I look at him.

I promised to live in obscurity, cross my heart.

Hope to die.

Instead I stand there on broil in instant lust with a man who is so scary there are no words.

Thank God Mitch speaks first. *Oh right, Mitch,* I remember in my dazed state.

"Castile." Mitch greets him tersely, his stormy eyes darkening.

"Maverick," the stranger named Castile drawls in return.

*Holy shit, they're, like, peeing in corners or something.* It's the perfect time for me to check out Mr. Friendly. I do, giving him a once-over and noticing that he certainly is built well, but that is not all. He has a presence, an indefinable quality.

I am the moth and he is the flame; his black eyes track me with quiet intensity.

I back up a step and Mitch frowns. "This is Jess Mackey." He introduces me reluctantly, and the dark stranger moves forward with a graceful stride that brings him uncomfortably close to me.

"Jess Mackey?" He cocks his head as if my name strikes some chord of recognition.

Of course, I know this is impossible. It doesn't matter; the breath of the suggestion causes my palms to dampen and his nostrils flare like he can scent my nervousness. *Danger up ahead*, my instincts scream.

I ignore those. "Yes," I mumble, "I'm Jess." I stick out the hand I just wiped on my jeans for him to shake and he looks at it curiously, then wraps his around mine.

It feels like a shock, a tingle; from the instant his skin touches mine it threads through me and lights my core with heat. His eyes widen minutely and Mitch clears his throat.

"Devin Castile," he says in a gravelly baritone.

I thought animal magnetism was bullshit. *Apparently not.*

I nod stupidly and he removes his hand, which was but moments before engulfing mine. His index finger trails for a split second over the delicate skin of the underside of my wrist and I shiver. His eyes darken with heat as he takes in my reaction.

The interchange takes seconds and I feel like it has undone me for all time.

Mitch looks between the two of us, licking his suddenly dry lips, and after an awkward pause he says, "Devin's a senior."

"A transfer, right, Mitch?" Devin asks in a tight voice.

"Yeah," Mitch says. "You know everyone, don't you, Castile?"

Devin Castile's gaze narrows on Mitch. "Pretty much. I like to know the head count . . . and besides, I wanted to meet your girlfriend," Devin says, adding, "She looks a little lost, if you ask me."

"No one did," Mitch says, his brows dropping like a brick above his eyes.

I know then I'll be late for my class as my face swivels from one to the other like a tennis match.

I turn to him and interject, "I'm not anyone's girlfriend." I'd survived two years in anonymity, I'm not blowing it now for insta-lust.

Devin doesn't turn to me when I state that. Instead he says to Mitch, "Just being friendly, Maverick, settle down."

*Friendly my ass,* I think.

Mitch's eyes narrow on Devin.

I back away; it's too much. It threatens my carefully orchestrated hiding. Two hot guys in the hall, sucking the available oxygen from my universe.

I'm having trouble breathing and about to be a gasping fish out of water at any moment.

They swivel to look at me at the same moment as a strangled noise escapes my tightly squeezed windpipe. I turn tail and briskly walk away.

I hear one of them call my name and one laugh.

I can bet which one is laughing at my cowardice.

I'm going to steer clear of him. Devin Castile is all sex and hotness wrapped up in a dangerous package.

I've worked hard to leave danger behind.

A few of the other students look up from their uninspired cafeteria meals when I stroll in but I ignore everyone, searching for Carlie. If I can't get this off my chest I think I'll die.

There she is, her dark curly hair bobbing in the lunch line, her iPod buds shoved in her ears.

I move up behind her and tap her shoulder; she turns with a smile, popping one of the buds out. "Hey, toots," she says, scooting the tray with the worst food in the world along on the metal rails, the earbud dangling dangerously above the jiggling Jell-O.

"So . . ." I look to my right and left and she smirks. "Remember that guy from the audition you forced me into?"

"I forced you into the guy?" She laughs.

I want to throttle her but restrain myself. "Y'know, the number guy," I hiss, slapping a carton of milk on my bright orange tray. "And you did *force me* into auditioning."

We move forward in the line and Carlie pops a straw for the milk in her mouth, chewing thoughtfully on it, picking up the tray with her other hand and sauntering off to our usual table.

I look around before the rest of our small group shows up. Carlie sits down and leisurely opens her milk and pushes the straw through the hole as I sit and fume. She sips. "Yeah, I remember him." She smirks again, then recites by memory: "Six foot two of pure love, dark hair, yummy sky-blue eyes . . .

*Actually, they're gray,* I think.

"And he groped your ta-ta, too," she says with snark.

"He didn't grope my tit, he was . . . positioning the number," I say, clarifying.

Carlie puts her carrot into her mouth in an obscene way and takes a loud chunk off the end with her perfect white teeth. I flinch a little at the crack as the carrot breaks.

"Jumpy," she says, sipping more milk.

"You're slaying me!" I say. "Can you listen?"

"No." Carlie preens. "You must first admit that you should have auditioned and how great of a friend I was to make you do so!" She holds up the amputated carrot and I burst out laughing.

Amber slaps her tray on the table, looks at me laughing at the carrot in the air and asks, "What did I miss?"

Carlie and I crack up. She can hardly keep the carrot in her mouth.

Carlie lets the cat out of the bag. "Jess here is having big-time sexual frustration in her tutu . . ."

*Gawd.* "No. That is *so* not it, Carlie . . . ya bitch!" I squeal, giving her a light smack on the arm.

"Anyway, she wants to do Number Boy," she says haughtily.

Amber gives Carlie a look and Carlie misses it. Oh shit—Carlie told Amber about Mitch. I glower at her.

Then I see Mitch is standing there and have ten kinds of cows on the spot. I am sure, with my hidden redhead's complexion, my skin is an attractive stop-sign red about now.

"Is this seat taken?" Mitch asks.

*I am so sure he heard all that.* "No." I stumble over the one word.

"No," Carlie drawls, finally waking up, "take a seat, lover." She pats the seat next to her and Mitch slides in, putting his tray there for our inspection, and gives Carlie a curious look.

I've never been so happy for the distraction of food in my life.

Amber, God love her, says, "So I hear you were in charge of the dancing hopefuls." She shamelessly bats her eyes at Mitch.

"Yeah," he says, taking a hand to the nape of his neck and rubbing like it's sore. Then he smiles, showing his dazzling white teeth. He aims a carefully neutral question my way. "You survived physics?"

I nod and Amber kicks my ankle. I give a small yelp and Mitch frowns. "Yes," I respond.

"Good," Mitch says, hiking his dripping pizza up to his mouth and taking an inhumanly large bite.

"Hungry, Mitch?" Carlie asks, winking at me.

He nods, missing her innuendo. "Yeah, I've got lacrosse later, got to fuel up."

Lacrosse. No wonder he's built like that, lean but broad of shoulder. I realize I'm staring and try to look away, pushing the lunch I no longer want to eat around on my plate.

*Come on, Jewell! Get a grip, you're not a blushing virgin,* I think, chastising myself. Yet, it has been so long since I've felt that delicious pressure, my body against another . . . well, I just can't go there mentally.

No men, no relationships, no connections. Maybe in a few years . . .

My mind interrupts my musings: *It's already been two years.*

I realize everyone's been staring at me. "What?" I ask.

"She's such a daydreamer," Carlie says, apologizing for me.

"Are you?" Mitch asks, wiping his mouth and tossing the napkin in the trash can.

"What?" I ask.

"A daydreamer?" he asks softly, and the question feels like a caress, loaded with something I can't name.

"Yes," I whisper honestly.

"Good," he says, standing as he swallows his milk in one gulp.

"Huh? Why?" I ask in confusion, craning my head to look up at him.

"I don't like planned people." Then his palms are on either side of my elbows, which are perched on the table. His gray eyes pierce my false blue ones.

"Meet me for coffee," he says. I can see from his intensity it isn't really a question.

"Where?" I hear myself asking.

"Java Head."

*Shit, that's where I work.* "All right," I say in agreement.

Mitch gives me the time to meet and slips out of the cafeteria.

"Girl!" Amber slaps the table and my untouched food bounces. "Can you . . . do you even know *how* to play hard to get? Have ya heard of that?"

"I don't think she's the one who's hard!" Carlie says, cackling.

*Oh my gawd,* I think in despair.

"So," Carlie says, and begins ticking imaginary points off on her fingertips. "You are going to be a prima ballerina"—she puts her left index finger to her right—"and you're finally gonna get laid," she says as she repeats the motion on her middle finger.

"Uh-huh, that's what I'm talkin' about, baby. Lay the pipe!" Amber says in a whisper that I'm sure carries to every table.

Before I can defend my position, establish a platform or whatever, they continue as if I'm not there.

"I say expand your horizons," Carlie says, and Amber mutters, "And other stuff."

I roll my eyes. I'm not keeping promises very well. Already I've lied to myself.

I have a couple of girlfriends I adore.

*And one that I lost.*

I promised there'd be no men.

*And now there is Mitch . . . and Devin Castile,* my mind whispers, like I need reminding, as I squelch that second name ruthlessly from my subconscious mutterings.

I put my head in my hands in defeat. I guess I'm giving in to life. It's like the ocean breaking against the rocks: it simply wears me down until I give in.

It was only a matter of time.

# THREE

~

The call comes and I pull the nail I've been massacring out of my mouth, trembling as I answer it. I always abuse my nails when I'm nervous.

And I am so nervous.

I'm one of five girls who have been selected for the spring integration program. It's a fledgling cooperative program that the U Dub has with Seattle Pacific Ballet. They have a touring artistic director who will ready us for an actual audition for the company, with a chance at a principal role. The thought of being a lead dancer with SPB is too surreal to contemplate. So I don't.

I'm not speaking with *the* Patrick Boel. No-oh. It's his assistant, but I am so excited the butterflies in that jar in my stomach have flown out long ago. They tremble with their silk wings inside me, caressing the tender underbelly of my emotions. For once it's not fear and intimidation but excitement and anticipation.

"May I speak with Jess Mackey?" a Tinker Bell voice trills on the line.

I'm still not used to my adopted name, even after two years, and pause for a fraction of a second before I answer, "Yes, this is she."

"I am phoning on behalf of Patrick Boel. Do you know who he is?"

*Hell yes I do.* "Yes," I answer out loud.

"Excellent." I hear a vague rustling of papers and I'm certain she's looking through notes or something else equally horrifying. She gives a delicate throat-clear and says, "Instructor Boel will expect you in the auditorium at four o'clock each afternoon for two hours' mandatory pointe work."

I die. I haven't been en pointe for two years. My feet are soft; my calluses have almost disappeared. I furiously grind through my mind looking for any response, my brain throwing up that I do have my old pointe shoes, thank God, because I could never stand the pain of breaking in a new pair.

"You *are* en pointe, Miss Mackey?" she asks with disdain. I think of the audition form that Carlie filled out for me, taking a hard, nervous gulp. How I don't know what boxes she checked and what ones she didn't. Knowing her, I bet she checked "yes" for all. Great.

I tell the second biggest lie in the last two years. "Of course."

"We cannot acquire dancers who have not had at least two years of pointe."

"Yes, I understand." *I do.*

"Excellent, Mr. Boel will be expecting you then."

"Yes, thank you," I say into the open line. Because his assistant, who didn't deign to give me her name, has hung up.

I shoot up off my bed and look at the sweaty leotard and tights that stick to my body, my two thick braids tacked into a bridge above my head, and see the clock reads five minutes until five.

Shit, I'm already late for coffee with Mitch.

I swoop into the shower and do a fifty-mile-an-hour job on my body, skip shaving and swipe mascara on my eyelashes while bouncing on one foot and throwing my flats on. I leave my ballet stuff piled on the floor, slamming the door on the way out.

I jog the entire way to my car, a little out of breath, all the while thinking I should have told Boel's assistant that I can't do it.

But I didn't want to say that. I *want* to do it. Even though it puts me at risk, I want to dance again. I smile to myself and jerk open the door of my beater Kia.

I jam the key in the ignition and give it a vicious twist . . . it doesn't start. I sit staring at it, willing it to come on, then I hit the steering wheel with the flat of my palm, and I give a yelp of pain, grabbing my hand with the other and putting them between my legs.

An engine comes to life beside me and I hear a kickstand hit the ground with a sharp tap.

I look up and Devin Castile sits on a bike.

Wow . . . just wow. Could this day get any more complicated?

His bike doesn't roar like an obnoxious storm but is what my horrible stepbrother would have termed a "quiet Harley." Devin looks over at me and our eyes meet.

He stands, leaving his bike running, and walks over to my shitty car and puts a hand on the roof. I watch his sleeve ride up, revealing a sculpted bicep with a black tattoo that twines up his arm like a snake. I suck in a breath, my hand still throbbing. I'm late for a date with a real, actual guy and here is *this* guy who makes every alarm bell I have, and ones I don't, go off. I lied about being en pointe and now I'm facing off with the spawn of Satan.

Devin studies me for a moment, saying nothing. Then the corners of his full mouth turn up slightly. "Need a ride . . . Jess?" he asks. Again I notice him using my name in an odd way.

"No," I say too quickly, shaking my head. He turns his head, his hair a shadow of black on a perfectly round skull. When I look closer, I see scars peppered over the surface, then he says, "Get out."

"No," I say, indignant. I'm not going to be bossed by a guy I met a day ago. *No matter how hot he is.*

He sighs, raking a hand over his trimmed skull. "Let me look at it."

"Oh," I say slowly. I slide out from behind the wheel and he folds himself into my car, his knees close to his chest. I giggle and he gives me a dark look, using the hand lever underneath the seat to make it go all the way back. Finally he fits.

Kinda.

He tries to turn it over and it protests. Finally, after some coaxing it buzzes to life. I watch him peer into the gauges.

The car dies.

"You know, Jess"—he spears me with his black gaze—"a car runs better if you put gas in it."

I run over there and stick my head in the car and my gas gauge reads zero.

*Wonderful, Jewell, way to go.* I turn my head and our faces are an inch away from meeting. Devin stays where he is, completely fine with our closeness; I rear back and hit my head hard on the underside of the top of the car.

I see stars and start to slip.

Devin catches me and I swear I go under for a second. Then suddenly I am very awake and in his arms.

The first thing I notice is how interesting a person's size can be. Devin Castile is a big guy. He is a huge guy when he's holding me. I feel small but not worthless. I feel whole and able—safe. An emotion that's been in short supply since as long as I can remember.

I blink, my feelings in a jumble and at the surface of me. "How tall are you?" I slur.

He smiles, brushing the hair that's escaped my damp bun out of my eyes in a gesture too tender for our superficial acquaintance.

"You really hit your head hard," he comments, and smiles, those white teeth contrasting with the duskiness of his skin tone.

He gathers me up and sets me slightly away from him.

The reality of where I need to be seizes me and I try to make it important in the soup of my brain. "I need to go!" I say, coming to my senses in pieces.

He cocks an inky brow. "Where? I'll take you."

My head swivels to the massive black bike, softly purring at the ready. I shake my head and it swims a little with the motion.

Suddenly, his huge hand wraps my elbow. "I said I'll take you." His eyes bore into mine. Commanding me.

I look at the bike, then at him, caving. "Okay."

He releases my elbow but looks ready to catch me again if I really do commit to passing out. "Where?" he repeats, already moving toward the bike.

"Java Head," I reply.

I don't tell him I have a date and he doesn't ask.

I slip behind him, searching around quickly for someplace to hang on, and Devin grabs my hands, moving them around the hardness of his flat belly. It's beyond awkward but necessary.

I give in as he turns and says, "Hang on."

He gives the throttle a vicious pump and lifts the kickstand as he pulls away in one fluid motion. Devin Castile is an economical man, with his words, with his movements.

Against every smart thing I promised myself, I find myself wondering how economical he'd be in bed.

He is a mystery and I discover I'm hanging on to my carefully cultivated indifference by the slimmest of margins.

We cruise through the University District, double-parking in front of metered slots that are filled with cars, the coffeehouse rising up against the sidewalk with great walls of glass.

I scramble off the back, feeling instantly more comfortable. There is just something about having your crotch plastered against the back of some hot guy that is beyond awkward.

At least against the back of Devin Castile it is. I don't analyze why it was awkward. I don't want to.

He stares at me for a minute as I smooth down hair that has tried to unravel from the tightish bun I threw it into.

Devin's gaze roams my body, beginning at my feet; he lingers over the parts men will, finally resting on my face. I swear he can see my skin jump over the pulse that beats at my throat. He smiles suddenly and my breath catches, the expression so utterly changes his face. "See ya, Jess."

He turns away, pulling out into traffic smoothly, becoming a dot of black leather in the distance.

I watch until he's out of sight and shiver.

But not from the cold.

It's the second time he's made me physically react to him, and this time he didn't even touch me.

I slowly turn away, going for the entrance of Java Head, and meet Mitch's eyes through the distorted glass of the window. He's seen the whole thing, his vantage point is both incognito but at the corner where the windows of glass meet and fold to wind the building.

*Shit-damn-shit.*

The bell tinkles as I slink inside and make my way between the tables. I notice Mitch has chosen a table at the farthest corner of the vintage-style coffeehouse. Actually, Java Head is housed in an antique building that has been converted for commercial use. The updated mechanicals of the building hang from the twenty-foot ceilings, exposed brick mixed with stainless steel, old moldings that have the residual paint of another century still framing the doorways and windows in a vintage rainbow of antiquity.

The staff call this table the "first-date table." I give a small laugh as I sit down and Mitch smiles in return.

"What's so funny?" he asks. His gray eyes are so pale they look almost white at this time of day. A trick of the light maybe.

"I work here," I say.

He lifts his dark brows and replies, "I know."

I frown in confusion. "You did? Well then . . ."

"I wanted to ask you to go somewhere familiar." He smiles again, spreading his palms away from his body. "You seemed shy. I didn't want to screw my chances by asking you to meet somewhere you didn't feel safe."

I scrunch up my nose. Is he like . . . totally amazing or a stalker?

Mitch laughs. "Let's get that look off your face!" His light eyes brim with humor.

"Ah . . . I do feel safe," I say, and realize I mean it.

We smile at each other.

His smile fades as he asks the question I wish he wouldn't: "I saw Castile brought you. I thought you didn't know him." His pale eyes gaze without guile into mine. Or presumed lack of guile. I notice he doesn't make a verbal note of my tardiness.

I flip the spoon that will stir my breve over and under, thinking. Finally, I blurt out the truth and find it makes me a little mad to feel like I have to explain myself. "My crappy car wouldn't start and he was there . . ."

"Ah," Mitch says, and I see tension ease out of his broad

shoulders. *If he knew what I thought of Devin, that wouldn't have eased him,* I think with a pang of guilt.

But he doesn't know. I don't either, not really. That doesn't mean that I don't want to flirt with finding out. I am circling a very dangerous new reality: losing my anonymity.

I'm still pretending to be Jess Mackey, Jewell MacLeod deliberately buried in a shallow grave. However, soon, I'll begin dancing again, I'm on a genuine date with La Hunk, a.k.a. Mitch Maverick, and I have a debilitating case of wet panties around Devin Castile.

Hiding in plain sight has just gotten a helluva lot harder.

Mitch stands, stretching, and his shirt rises, giving me a teasing sliver of abs. His eyes meet mine, his arms coming to rest again by his sides. "What's your poison?"

*My oh my, he has interesting phrasing.* I can't keep the smile back as my internal smart-ass quips at everything he says. Out loud I reply, "Breve with sugar-free caramel."

"Don't get that sugar-free shit, it's damn bad for you."

"Okay . . . Dad," I drawl, and I see heat take up residence in those pale eyes as he continues to stare at me. Mitch reaches toward me and cups his large hand on my jaw, the loose cradle causing warmth to spread from the point of contact. He gives a small caress with his thumb. "Not. Having. Dad. Thoughts," he says, then adds, "Nope!" He winks and drops his hand from my hot skin. A flush rises, heating my face, and I feel the weight of his observation as he walks away, my eyes scoping his tight ass in jeans that fit him just right.

I give a hard swallow and turn away from his broad back as he orders, looking out into the street, the pedestrians scurrying to whatever place calls to them, needs them. My eyes scan the deep blue of the October sky, Indian summer in full throttle. I look down at my flats and skinny jeans, my lightweight sweater having slid off one shoulder, and know that my days of wearing lightweight clothes are numbered.

I froze on the short ride on the back of Devin's bike.

I wouldn't trade the ride for anything. I know I'm playing a dangerous game with two men. One seemingly perfect and the other impossible to ignore. If living through Thad's jealous rages and anger over my perceived favoritism in the family has taught me anything, it is to seize every good thing that I can, however fleeting.

My chin is in my palm and I'm a million miles away when Mitch returns with the steaming and fully foamed breve, the rich smell of coffee causing me to sigh with comfort. There's just something about my favorite brew that gives me a happy flutter of contentment. The small daily pleasures of life separate us from the animals, soundly rescuing my humanity for another day of life worth living. I see Toby, the cashier, give me a nod as I take my first sip and I give a small wave in acknowledgment. He works a different shift than me but all of us coffee compatriots know each other.

"Thank you," I murmur, that small package of happiness a gift. Mitch sees its effect when our fingers brush as he transfers the cup to my hand, his eyes flicking to mine as I cast mine down.

"So . . . you're a dancing girl," Mitch says by way of breaking the ice.

Wrong move, but a normal one. He doesn't know I'm hiding from a psychotic relative.

I nod in a noncommittal way and he gives a bemused smile back, easily seeing my lack of details.

I lean forward, wrapping both hands on the hot cup, the sleeve allowing my fingers to warm there instead of burn. "What about you? Why are you the number guy?"

I realize my mistake the instant I say it and he grins. He now has absolute confirmation that he's the one Carlie was referencing at lunch a few days ago. Special.

Mitch lets me off the hook, spinning his cup. How he downed that entire hot coffee in zero point five seconds is a complete mystery. "Lacrosse players are required to perform 'civic duty'"—he makes air quotes—"for cross-related sports."

"Ballet is not technically a sport," I reply, taking a small sip of my cooling but still delicious froth of coffee.

Mitch's lips lift in a smirk. "There are those who would argue that, but since you're the one who said it first . . ." He throws up his palms in self-defense and I laugh.

"There's way too much finesse required for ballet to be anything less than the finest example of athletic prowess. *Sport* is not a strong enough term," I say, clarifying.

Mitch gives a low whistle. "How are your English skills, Jess?"

I've messed up and know it. I cannot let my upbringing peek through my carefully constructed façade. I hide my nervousness with another deliberate sip of coffee, formulating a careful response.

"I do okay." I laugh dismissively. I knew those years of being a senator's daughter, albeit only by marriage, marked me in ways that others can't pinpoint but will note.

I don't want to be noteworthy.

Mitch grows thoughtful, then says, "There's something different about you, Jess. I can't put my finger on it." He hesitates. "But I like it," he says, and I let out the breath I didn't realize I was holding.

"Tell me about Jess Mackey," Mitch says. Those pale eyes meet mine as he aimlessly spins the empty cup with a finger. My palms sweat. I take deep breaths that let me settle my nervousness. If I'm to date, really and truly begin to live, I have to give it a go.

"Well . . . I dance," I say, thinking that's safe since he clearly knows that.

Mitch gives a soft chuckle, flipping his brown hair out of his eyes. "Clearly . . . but what else?"

I cast my eyes down, thinking. Finally I answer with as much truth as I have to give. "I'm making a fresh start here. I thought the dance audition was as good as any place to start."

"Doesn't look like you were that into auditioning to me . . ." Mitch trails off, keeping me engaged with that light gray gaze.

*Busted.* "No," I laugh and he smiles. "It's Carlie's fault. She . . . made me." My fingers go to my dancer's knot at my nape, nervously tightening it.

"But now you're happy?" he asks as if he's not sure.

"Not yet, but it's a start." I smile at Mitch to take the bite out of my words, but it never totally leaves them.

Mitch reaches across the table and takes my hand; my

fingers are chilled. *Cold hands, warm heart,* I think randomly. "Not all of us have the best start," he says, releasing my hand and leaning back in the chair until it almost touches the rough brick of the wall. "Take me," he says, thumb at his chest, and I feel my brows rise. I'm infinitely more comfortable discussing him than myself as I feel the tension in my shoulders ease. "I got a full ride to the U Dub because of lacrosse. It's certainly not based on academic." His eyes narrow down like lasers on me and my heart does a slow flip. "But you, Jess . . ." he spreads his palms out, "you've been given something . . . that special . . ." he palms his chin, thinking. When he snaps his fingers I can't stop the flinch. "Spark," he says in a low voice, full of meaning, impact. I look down, my fingers clasped together.

"Thanks," I say, meeting his gaze, though I don't want to; compliments always make me squirm. Mitch seems to sense my discomfort.

"So," he asks, grabbing my cup and standing. "Did we solve the problems of the world?"

I shake my head, wisps of hair fluttering with the movement. I notice night has fallen, that two hours have gone by without my knowing it.

"No?" His brows pop. "We have time for that . . ." Those translucent eyes bore into mine. "Meet me for dinner," he commands, taking the hand that is now free of a cup.

As our flesh connects, my heart speeds and I look up into his face, the butterflies in my tummy begging for release, my soul crying for freedom.

I know it's a terrible mistake.

I say yes anyway.

Jess Mackey wants to see this man.

Jewell MacLeod wants to be free.

It's an irresistible combination.

I don't realize it at the time but there is always a cost with freedom.

# FOUR

"*What* is that?" I ask, pointing, and Mitch laughs self-consciously, moving a hand through his hair just as the meter clicks to *expired*.

*He fed the meter for two hours and it's hungry again,* I think.

Is it flattering or presumptuous that he assumed the length of our date? I know that I'm splitting hairs, trying to find fault with the perfect distraction of our time together. Well, almost perfect; I *was* dropped off by Devin Castile.

"It's my weakness, Jess." He strokes a finger down the flank of his vintage car like it's a lover and I actually feel a pang of jealousy. Mitch is a step away from calling the car by a female name. I can tell; he has that look.

He sees my face and laughs, a rich throaty sound that makes me smile despite myself. "It's a 1974 LT1 Camaro," he says in an I-get-dreamy-over-vehicles voice. I suppress an epic eye-roll.

I just want mine to start, thank you very much. That's the extent of my concern over cars.

"So, it's a vintage car and . . ." I move my palm in the direction of the off-white car, a chocolate racing stripe beginning at the hood and finishing with a lick on the back spoiler, trying to rustle up the obligatory excitement. *So isn't happening.*

I shake my head, putting a hand to my chest. "I'm the girl who got a ride with Devin because I ran out of gas."

Mitch looks at me and I suddenly feel bad for mentioning Castile.

He gives a subtle shrug, not picking up on the reference. Point for Mitch. I'm fooling myself; all girls keep score.

He opens the door and I lie down in the seat. At least, that's what it feels like. The car's built low to the ground, and the seat's in a semi-reclined position automatically.

Mitch turns the key in the ignition and the powerful engine roars to life. I watch him touch the shifter that is located between the seats, but it's an automatic. His powerful hands wrap around the eight ball he's replaced the original grip with and I feel a smile form at the subtle sense of humor in that choice.

I watch him pull away and I stiffen when he asks a question I'm sure he's been mulling over: "Where did you say you're from?"

*I didn't.* "Iowa," I lie, hoping that's the end of it. Of course it isn't.

He puts on his blinker and I automatically calculate the time before I'm at the dorms.

Five minutes. *I can get through that,* I think.

"I hear a little accent," he says, and I let the silence speak for me. Mitch catches me off guard with, "How long have you danced in bal-let?" he asks, pronouncing it like I do. Differently. Regionally differently, and I realize he's sniffing. How come Mitch is more interested in getting to know me than getting into my panties?

Not that it isn't the greatest thing ever. I want a guy to want me and *want* me. It's not that a vibrator isn't a great invention, but it isn't the real McCoy. Not only are the first-date inquiries getting a little old, they make me as nervous as a cat in a room full of rockers. But I don't just want a one-night stand either.

Girls are complicated creatures and I fit right into that mold.

I sigh and his eyes flick to mine. Not answering was an alert; answering is almost as bad. I answer.

"My mom enrolled me when I was four," I say. When he says nothing, his eyes on the road, I continue. "But when I became a teenager, they thought I might get too tall for ballet." I look down at my clenched hands, thinking about my parents ranting at me to keep my weight down. Who was going to partner someone they couldn't lift? That made me think about Thad and his unhealthy interest in my physique; it was part of his intimidation to secure my continued silence. Silence secured by threats. I'd been unwitting witness to his cruelty as evidenced in the corpses of the innocent animals that were unlucky enough to live within the proximity of the monster my stepbrother was. Is. I kept his secrets out of fear. And look at where that put me. Faith is dead because of confidences I spilled, hiding because I don't want to end up like the animals . . . or worse.

I swallow and continue. "Anyway, I guess I was lucky and topped out shorter."

"You're not short," Mitch says casually. I know that at five foot six, I'm not short, but I'm a little on the tall side for ballet. If I was en pointe, my partner would need to be five feet ten. Most male ballet dancers are built more like gymnasts and less statuesque. They have powerful bodies that are low to the ground, not generally tall.

"No," I say softly, sighing with relief as I see the university dorm rise past the swell of the manicured grounds of the University of Washington. It's quite old, mid nineteenth century.

He pulls into a parking spot and turns the car off.

"Who made you hate talking about yourself?" Mitch asks, turning his body at the waist, the streetlight shadowing everything but those glacial eyes.

*Pick one.* "No one," I say. I think quickly. "My family is reserved," I explain.

"Are you close to them?"

*Shit-damn-shit.* "No . . ." I pause. "I don't have any siblings and my parents are . . . distant." I almost laugh at that; *distant* doesn't even begin to cover it. The sibling thing doesn't feel like a lie at all; it comforts me to put Thad in that category: Non-relative.

Mitch doesn't say anything to my hastily contrived background, which is a relief. That's the trouble with lying; it's challenging to keep everything straight.

Instead, he moves his hand to the many wisps of hair that have escaped my bun, and twisting them together, he makes a small rope of my dark blond hair and tucks it behind my ear. "You don't wear your hair down," he says, and I shake my head.

I know Mitch will kiss me as he leans forward and I meet him, our lips coming together. Then they are seeking, his mouth moving across mine with the softest press of skin, like breath and air. My heart picks up its pace and I fall into the steady suck and tease of his mouth as his large hand wraps around me, pressing me closer.

When my knee hits the gearshift I laugh, his tongue against my teeth, and he smiles against my mouth. The windows are fogged up and I slide back in my seat, where I watch Mitch slow his panting to a regular breathing pattern.

"That was nice," he says, blatant heat fills his expression telling me it could have been more if I wanted it. The knowledge stands in those light eyes, the invitation as well.

I know I'm not ready.

I nod, then do something spontaneous. I draw a small heart on the foggy window glass.

I open the door and get out, his eyes pegged on the heart I made on the car window. I stick my head inside the saunalike interior, our innocent kiss having changed that small sliver of atmosphere to what it is right now: heated and evolving. The relationship has grown beyond the innocence of friendship and become something more. Complicated. I'm at once exhilarated by this taste of freedom I've allowed myself and scared that I've made the concession.

"Dinner?" he asks with a smile, the warmth of our make-out session dissipating like smoke up a flue.

I nod again, closing the door.

I walk to my dorm, oblivious to eyes that watch my progress with the premeditation of a predator.

~

I stir the Hershey's syrup into the glass, watching the stripe of chocolate get sucked up in the whirlpool of white.

Carlie makes a gagging noise. "That's gonna go right to your ass. I'm just sayin'."

I grin. "It's the drink of the gods. Besides," I say, going up en pointe, balancing the milk glass perfectly, "I need all the calories I can get."

Carlie rolls her dark eyes. "I thought you said you were worried about being light enough."

I come down gracefully, the lamb's wool in my pointe shoes shifting to accommodate the movement, and I sit on the edge of my bed, keeping my toes en pointe. "I am borderline . . ." I shrug but feel that telltale nervousness flood my belly in an uncomfortable surge, curdling the chocolate milk I'm drinking.

I let my hands dangle between my knees, setting the glass between my feet, which remain in perpetual pointe.

"I wasn't saying you were fat," Carlie says, backpedaling as she eyes me. "Shit, girl, you're too thin as it is."

I'm really a marginally good weight for ballet. One hundred ten would be better; I'm living with the one hundred fifteen I'm at now.

"I'll be fine. Once I begin the workouts with Boel, that extra bit will come right off."

"This extra bit," Carlie says, smirking as her hands grab her huge tits and jerk them up by her throat.

I cackle at her. I still have boobs, so not all is lost.

She laughs. "You need a decent tit trap," she says, then adds, "I have some . . ."

I shake my head. "One, you're in the Oh My God section of the bra store . . . ," I say. Then, "And however much I appreciate your offer, I'll have to get my own . . ."

"Tit trap," Carlie repeats, grinning. "Now, ballet girl. Tell me about La Hunk."

I blush and she catches it.

"What?" she nearly shrieks. "Did he pet the kitty?"

"No!" I say, my face growing hotter, if that's possible. "We just kissed . . ."

Carlie taps her foot. She definitely wants the goods.

"Okay," I say, giving up. "We kissed, but I have to tell you what happened with Devin Castile."

"*The* Devin Castile?" she asks.

I feel the furrow form between my eyes.

"Yeah . . . unless there's some other intense dude in leather who skulks around."

Carlie slowly nods. "I know him."

Her lack of comment tells me a buttload. None of it good.

"What is it?" I ask, thinking how stupid it was for me to get a ride with him. How he's a stranger to me.

A powerful one.

"He's so hot, there's no doubt. I'd do him . . . ," she says, and I roll my eyes. If it was six feet, muscled, with a dangling dick, Carlie would be *so* there.

"What?" she asks, then gives a sheepish smile. Her gaze meets mine. "I've just heard some smack about him."

My frown deepens.

"There's a few chicks who say he likes it rough."

*What?* My mind skitters over the memory of his tenderness as he held me. *Rough what?*

"Catch a clue, ballet girl," Carlie says, reading my puzzled expression. "He likes to do 'em and leave 'em. And it doesn't much matter where. A wall, a car, the elevator . . ." She shrugs.

"We're not talking the R-word here?" I whisper with barely contained revulsion, my sensory memory giving a hiccup as my windpipe threatens to narrow. I breathe evenly and deeply twice, heading off the semi panic attack successfully.

Carlie quickly shakes her head.

"I hear a *but* . . . ," I say, wanting to flesh this out.

"I think a few didn't know what they were doing; they bit off more than they could chew. You feel me?"

An image of Carlie crunching on the carrot rises in my mind and I laugh.

"This is kinda serious."

"I just thought about you and vegetables, and I don't know . . ." I grin and giggle helplessly.

"Nice, ya tart," Carlie says, trying to act mad and fold her arms, huffing. I don't fall for it for one minute.

"So, Devin Castile will do halfway-willing girls?" I say as a point of clarity. "But it's consensual?" I ask, mentally crossing him off a list I didn't realize I was consulting.

Kind of confusing. *Kind of intriguing,* I admit. Then I think of Mitch. He seems so much safer. Regulated.

That works for me.

"I just think your prissy ass should stick with Mitch. He's . . ."

"Safe." I finish her thought and she nods.

"He's cute too." Carlie sounds like she's convincing me.

We stare at each other for a few moments.

"You're dying to screw Castile, aren't ya?"

I think about lying. *Yeah.* "Maybe," I say.

"I was afraid of that," Carlie says, then perks up. "I think we'll devise an Operation Avoid Castile."

*Brilliant.* A new scheme by Carlie. I give her the look she deserves for conjuring shit up as usual.

She rolls her eyes at me. "Listen, you don't seem like his type, 'kay?" Carlie meets my eyes. "He can't possibly want to bother with you," she says, sweeping her hand down my lean dancer's physique. I'm wearing my standard unattractive leotard and tights, my long, thick hair wound in my standard braid crown.

I think about the way Castile looks at me and shiver. Just remembering the way it feels to have his eyes on my body, my face.

It carries weight.

"Shit," Carlie breathes, studying my kaleidoscope of expressions. "He wants to do you?"

I look at her miserably and nod. "I think so."

"Well, you're not Miss Confidence, so if you think it's a possibility . . . I'll take that as gospel fact."

Carlie stands and I move to the barre, finishing my exercises as she paces.

I begin deep pliés, not breaking the fluidity of the

movement except to extend my arm and then sweep it back down to graze the floor with my hand.

"I think we need to start right away. You're gonna show Castile that you mean business with the other guy. Let La Hunk hanging off you like a cheap suit give him the message. He'll back down. He's smokin' hot; he's not gonna keep after your dancing ass when he can have one of the one hundred point one sluts that'll spread their knees for any swinging prick with a pulse." She shrugs and I bark out a laugh, screwing my last dip six ways to Sunday.

"Right," I say in a droll tone, "I'll just do 'La Hunk' and then Castile will forget me." I can barely keep a straight face. I give up and burst out laughing.

"It's better than old faithful," Carlie says, making a circle with her left hand and stabbing the index finger of her other hand through the hole.

My eyes stray to my lockbox and I giggle. "True . . . but . . ."

Carlie pegs her hands on her curvy hips, tossing her dark curly hair over her shoulder. "Okay, I know you feel uncomfortable talking about your past."

I stiffen and she throws her hand out. "See? You don't trust me!" Carlie says.

I stave off the old argument smoothly. "I haven't had sex in over two years, so I feel . . ." *Shy, incompetent, undesirable . . . unwanted, scared.* "Out of practice."

Carlie momentarily forgets that I never talk about myself or say anything about my past and grins. "So practice." Her eyes glitter with humor. "Offer it up, Jess. I bet you Mitch Maverick will jump on you."

*Perfect . . . or not.* "I don't know," I say, spinning in the center of the room.

"How come you don't puke?" Carlie asks, watching me before finally turning away.

"I spot my corner."

"Riiiight," Carlie drawls, then asks, "When do you start the dance-o-matic?"

I stop, landing in third position, and lower my arms. "Tomorrow."

"You have to wear those?" She points to my toe shoes, beaten so hard the pink satin looks vaguely gray at the edges, my arch true and full while en pointe.

"After warm-ups."

Amber bursts into the room.

We look at her, startled.

"There's been another one," she says, her beautiful golden eyes scattered and wide. We're both blank for a few seconds.

Then it hits us. We don't ask; we know.

Another girl taken. Carlie and I look at each other in mutual horror. I gather my stuff together to hit the dorm showers. The lighthearted talk of screwing guys and ballet practice pales beside the news there's been another victim of violence in the school.

"It was Amanda," Amber says, and my stomach instantly gives a slow, heated roll. Carlie's eyes find mine. She knows what violence against women does to me. She's never asked; she's just that intuitive.

Someday I'll tell Carlie the truth. But that day isn't now.

Amanda was in my biology class.

"How?" I ask.

Amber responds, "The usual: on campus, during regular school hours, at night."

"Is there . . . a . . . body?" Carlie queries.

"Not yet."

What Amber doesn't say is there always is one . . . eventually.

They'll find a body and we'll all go back to being scared, a repeat of freshman year but worse. Some stalker was plucking out the plums of the female population and there was no correlation of commonality other than their gender and age that the police could determine at this point.

I gather my things for showering, clutching my towel and toiletries tighter against my chest. I can't help the image of Thad that springs to mind. It seems like the unexplained murders have a feel of a slow spiral, a whirlpool effect. And guess who's dead-center? It's not fair for me to lump this in with what I know about my stepbrother. But somehow, that portentous foreboding doesn't loosen its hold on me.

"I'm . . . going to go shower," I say to Amber and Carlie, and Carlie nods, the wind taken out of her sails as we exit my dorm room, which is little better than a closet. I opted for a nonshared room without a bath. Sharing a room and getting a bathroom or having a single room and a communal bathroom. Not a hard choice for me.

I don't need any roommates. Living a lie will zap the energy right out of you.

We part ways, all of us contemplating another year of fear and our fragile safety.

I'm already watchful.

A certain level of paranoia is normal for me; what difference does more make?

I clutch my towel and toiletries to my chest, deep in thought.

When I round the corner I plow into a muscular chest and gasp as strong hands engulf my shoulders, my shower stuff sliding to a pile at my feet.

It's Brock from biology. Instant fear coils in my belly like a snake seeking a target, the conversation of the missing coed nipping at the heels of my thoughts.

"Going somewhere?" he asks, his fingers biting into my shoulders.

I jerk my upper body out of his hands.

He lets me go. I couldn't have gotten away if he wanted to keep me. We stare at each other for a heartbeat. "The bathroom," I answer in a low voice. "Now, move out of my way." I muster a bravado I don't feel.

He leans toward me and reminds me so acutely of Thad for a moment that I have a sense of vertigo that begins at my feet and works its way up to my head in a heated rush of sick dizziness.

"Take your hands off her . . . Brock," a voice says, clipping his name like a swear word.

I know the timbre of that voice.

Brock flicks his eyes behind my head and responds, "Fuck off, Castile. Jess and I were just . . . talking." His hands are back on my shoulders with bruising force. He turns me to face Castile.

Then Brock whispers in my ear, "Don't fuck this up."

Devin looks utterly at ease, his unhurried gaze traveling down our connected limbs. The hot line of Brock is against my back, his fingers digging . . . digging into my shoulders. The sweat from my workout chills with the fear and strain my body is undergoing with his nearness.

"Do you want to *talk*, Jess?" Devin asks. "Do you want to be held by him?"

*Held by him?* I wonder, my fear and confusion making my brain grind through responses.

However, it's Brock who tears the involuntary response out of me. He squeezes me and I can't keep the hurt inside my body.

I've had many years of practice but have grown rusty, apparently.

A small, pained sound escapes my lips as I breathe out, "No."

Castile moves like wicked liquid lightning, jabbing a punch right into Brock's forehead, an easy target as Brock is six feet plus, his head dwarfing mine.

He begins to topple like a mighty tree and I fall with him.

Devin tears me out of his arms and puts me behind his body protectively.

Brock staggers backward, his forehead split and bleeding, and launches himself at Devin.

Brock's head rocks back as Devin slams his fist into Brock's jaw, and he falls on his ass in a tangle of his own arms and legs.

"Don't get up, Brock," Castile murmurs in an even voice, crouched, with his fists riding high and tight next to his jaw.

My face is buried in Devin's back, my fingers locked and chilling with the force of my grip against the smooth leather.

Forever the smell of leather will bring me comfort. It's a basic fact that scent is the strongest memory trigger, and Devin Castile's saving me from Brock has gotten all wrapped up in the back of a leather jacket heated with his scent. His protection.

This man couldn't be the pervert that Carlie made him out to be.

Yet, he is undoubtedly violent.

I peek around him, seeing Brock's hate for me shining from his position on the floor.

Devin saved me.

He's also marked me.

I see it in Brock's eyes. He's been emasculated and I'm bearing witness to his embarrassment, and Brock won't soon be forgetting it.

I am now a target, and I move my face away from his line of sight.

I take a deep, shuddering breath and think of how dangerous my life has suddenly become.

I wonder for the second time that day if the predator I know is better than the predator I don't.

I think of Faith.

As I stand behind Devin Castile, inhaling the smell of warm leather and maleness, I finally decide I'd rather live with the potential than the reality.

# FIVE

*My* hands won't stop shaking and Devin covers them with his own, my eyes rising to meet his.

I am so in trouble here.

We look at each other for a moment, then I look away from his intense inspection to see where Brock is. I watch his palm slap the wall to brace him as he stands. He pinches his nose to stanch the flow of blood. Brock's eyes meet mine with a glare of hatred that is so powerful I flinch. His eyes flick to Devin, who stands quietly by my side, and whatever he sees there convinces him to leave.

While he still can.

He stomps down the corridor and we watch him exit. I breathe deeply and exhale a puff of air frosting as we move out of the corridor to the outside and remove ourselves from the event that just happened. I breathe easier getting out of there, that claustrophobic feeling abating.

"What happened?" Devin asks, still holding my cold hands in his.

I gently extract them and he gives a little tilt at the corners of his mouth. I am so not comfortable touching him.

I lift a shoulder. "I don't know, he's pissed because Brad put him in his place last week in biology."

"Gunner?" Devin asks, his brow cocked.

I nod but frown. "Do you know everyone?"

"Just about," he says. "But not you."

We stare at each other some more, the silence growing uncomfortable. Finally, I break it. "I don't think he liked getting dressed down in front of me."

Devin's brows come together. I thought his eyes were nearly black, but they're actually a deep root beer color, rich chocolate washed by amber.

They're beautiful, lined by sooty black lashes that curl slightly. No mascara for him. I give a laugh at the thought of Devin in makeup and his eyes narrow. "What's so funny? Didn't I just interrupt an extreme manhandle there?"

I shake my head (I'm not answering that) and cover my mouth, still trembling slightly after the encounter with Brock. You know how it is when you try not to laugh and can't stop. That's becoming my problem. And I know part of it is the trauma of what just happened . . . and being this close to Castile.

"You gotta watch him," Devin said, his eyes straying to the corridor where Brock disappeared. "He's got a rep. And now he'll be all ass-hurt because I stopped him from threatening you."

"Well, it's not like he was going to get a date with the way he went about it!" I laugh, folding my arms across my chest, and Devin stares at my breasts in a leisurely way. When he reaches out to touch my shoulder I cringe and he ignores me, moving away the lightweight sweater I threw on over my ballet gear. I needed it when my body cooled after my exercises; it's chilly outside.

He studies the skin there, bringing gooseflesh to the surface with his touch.

His eyes meet mine. "You'll bruise . . . *that bastard.*" Devin's hands drop and clench into fists. "He needs a real beat-down."

My mouth twitches. "Was that a fake one?"

His eyes don't waver from mine, my comedy lost in the depths of his gaze.

He moves toward me, contained violence in motion, backing me up against the wall, the courtyard bare of students at this odd time of day, between meals, after class, sports students not yet finished.

I let him, my heart speeding. "What are you doing?" I ask. *But I know.*

With one of his hands on either side of my body, I'm caged. The brick façade of the dorm leaches cold through my leotard, the sweat of my workout chilling it further.

Devin studies my upturned face, his eyes cannibalizing me with heat, with want. But instead of giving in to what I see there, he trails a finger down from my temple to my jaw, cupping it loosely. Then he answers my question.

"What I should have done the moment I saw you with Maverick," he says, his lips hovering above mine. They are so close I can feel the heat of his skin; I imagine the stubble that I saw on that square jaw rasping against me in places he hasn't explored.

"May I kiss you, Jess?" he whispers above my mouth.

*No.* "Yes," I whisper back against every impulse not to.

He doesn't take my lips softly but crushes my mouth against his, a storm crashing into the shore, his full lips working over mine, forcing them open, and I groan as he gathers me against him, his huge hands splaying against my lower back in a convulsive surge, bringing me into the line of his body.

"Respond," he commands in a low growl.

His verbal demand brings a primal coil of heat that begins at my wet G-string and tingles in an unending ripple of electric sensation, flowing to the tips of my fingers.

*Oh God.*

Devin raises his hand and cups my breast underneath the light sweater while his body presses me under the eaves of my dorm building. A man I hardly know has me against him and has rolled my nipple in a move so smooth I never saw it coming, the sensitive bundle of nerves a thread pulling the heat from my core and tethering the two on a taut line like an erotic electric switch flipped.

I gasp, throwing my head back. "Stop," I breathe, not wanting his hand off me. Ever.

"Your body says yes," he says against my skin, his mouth buried in that soft area of the neck all females possess. "I taste your sweat, your sweetness . . . ," he says as his hand leaves my breast and walks its way down my rib cage.

Lower.

My panties flood with moisture in anticipation, my sex throbbing. I know he's going to touch me and a huge part of me wants it. A small part of me that's unraveled from the run-in with Brock rebels. My body squelches it easily. I'm going to let him finger me in public; I haven't had sex in over two years and Devin has undone my resolve in five minutes.

"Get off her!" Mitch says.

I jerk back from Devin and try to scramble away, my leotard rasping on the rough brick. I can feel the heat of my embarrassment suffuse me from head to toe. I want to die.

Where the hell is a handy rock to climb underneath when ya need one? I give a soft groan, and not the excited kind, the mortified type.

"What's going on here?" Mitch asks, his eyes shifting from Devin to me.

*Shit—déjà fucking vu,* I think.

"I . . . ," I begin to say miserably.

"I was tonguing your girlfriend, Maverick," Devin says casually, wrapping me against the side of his body.

*Oh sweet baby Jesus.*

Mitch looks at Devin in disgust. "You fuckup." He looks at me, dismissing Devin, and I cringe from the betrayal I see there. One date and he owned me, I guess.

"You're with Castile now? Seriously?" Mitch asks, and I get pissed.

"No," I say, shoving Devin away. He pretends to stagger, putting a hand over his heart. "He . . . Brock tried to threaten me and Devin . . ."

All the events come crashing down on my head: the creeper

who killed Amanda, Brock accosting me in the hall and, when I was at my most emotionally vulnerable point, Devin lighting the fire of that spark between us as surely as a match to kindling. I cover my face with my hands.

And now, like a cherry on top of the misery cake, Mitch Maverick, a.k.a. La Hunk, thinks I'm a whore who would let some strange guy feel me up in public.

And he isn't wrong. *What was I thinking?*

I run into the building, scooping up the towel and toiletries I dropped when Brock laid his hands on me.

"Jess, wait . . . ," Mitch says, regret lacing his words.

"Don't mess with her," I hear Devin say.

"Get your fucking hands off me," Mitch says.

I shut the dorm bathroom door, pressing my back against its solidness, clenching my eyes against the last half hour.

I can hear loud voices outside and I ignore them, floating toward the mirror.

I stare back at myself.

Jewell MacLeod stares back.

A girl with dark blond hair that's really a rich auburn. Blue eyes bore into the glass, with green ones lurking underneath the guise of contacts.

I take my sweater off and see livid fingerprints where Brock held me, and I shiver.

Devin held me harder but his touch didn't leave bruises.

I shiver, not from fear or cold, but from the memory of the press of his body through the denim he wore, his dick rolling between the folds of what my leotard barely covered.

I stare at my reflection for a while.

When the light dwindles to twilight I turn away with a sigh. Stripping off my gear, I walk naked into the tiled stall; a row of six nozzles greets me and I travel to the end. My shower shoes smack the tiled surface with an echo that only barely wet tile makes.

I stand underneath the hot spray and think about Devin, my body aching to finish what he began, a low pulse of residual desire my constant companion.

I think about Mitch. No matter what, the kiss that Devin gave me eclipsed Mitch's. I can't even remember what it was like. I sigh, tilting my head back and letting the warm water run into my mouth and slide down my scalded skin in rivulets.

Last, I think of Brock and why he has fixated on me. Maybe I'll tell Brad. Maybe I won't.

I will be avoiding two men: Mitch Maverick and Devin Castile.

Especially Castile.

I arrive for ballet at fifteen until four. I'm not going to have *the* Patrick Boel meet me and have lack of punctuality to add to the list. No. I press my pointe slippers into an arch, then straighten them. I repeat the process a few times. I left my damp shoes on the clanking and hissing radiator in my room to let the heat soften them; perspiration mixed with the steam will make the arches more malleable.

They stink vaguely like sweat and copper. I've bled in these shoes.

I walk out into the huge auditorium and stop. Four other dancers stand around in a loose circle, many with one knee up, a toe en pointe, while they visit nervously. Then they switch to the other toe; equal billing.

I move toward them, the final dancer. I feel like I am finally seeing light at the end of a long, dark tunnel. I study them and see that everyone has their hair slicked back from their face except me. Mine is braided tightly against my head, tails crossed and pinned.

They quiet as I approach.

"Hi," I say.

No one says a word. Ballerinas are notoriously competitive and I am no exception. However, introductions won't derail our performances.

I sigh, ready to insert myself regardless, when I hear a sharp clap behind me.

It's Patrick Boel.

*He's built like a brick shithouse!* Yet he moves so gracefully I stare well past the point of rudeness.

"Dancers," he says by way of introduction. When all of us intimidated girls nod, he continues, a graceful palm sweeping toward our general location. "Two of you will be removed from my presence today." His hazel eyes meet mine. "I do not tolerate lazy, fat, clumsy or otherwise subpar dancers."

I gulp. It seems that his words are meant for me and me alone. His piercing gaze roves our forms, missing nothing.

He approaches a very short girl. She is a perfect size for ballet: five feet one and maybe ninety-ish pounds. "Too short, too clumsy . . . too fat, you are excused," Patrick Boel says, and my palms dampen.

If he thinks her too fat and short, *what must he think of me?*

Only true grit keeps me anchored to the spot, my stomach churning with thoughts of my imminent dismissal.

He reaches out with a snakelike precision mixed with the elegance of an antelope and grabs my thigh. I jump but he holds me. "How much do you dance each day?" he asks so casually that I blurt out the truth: "Two hours."

He slaps my thigh and the sting brings tears to my eyes. "Make it four . . . Jess," he says, meeting my eyes. My eyes widen at my realization that my dance instructor has done as much research on us as I have on him.

"Yes, Mr. Boel," I say, resisting the urge to comfort my thigh with my hand, and he knows it, a smile ghosting his lips, then disappearing. He does a different thing to each dancer. The dwarf dancer's dismissal rings in all our heads. I can still hear her tears echoing in my mind and she's been gone five minutes.

"Any other volunteers who wish to relieve themselves of my tutelage?"

We shake our heads.

"Fine." He smiles.

By the end of our practice two more girls have quit, leaving myself and one other. I can feel a new blister burst once I move across the auditorium, snapping my head to the corner, my feet screaming from the different abuse Boel puts me through, my body shaking from exhaustion.

"Enough!" Boel fumes, stalking back and forth, and I release from spinning, landing into third, the other dancer coming to rest beside me. She gives me a nervous look and shakes her head slightly. We're the smartest of the group. We don't talk, we just perform like his puppets.

He is the master and we are the slaves.

Dancing slaves.

"You"—he points at the other dancer—"move like you must instead of with desire. Again."

She spins off and I control my breathing as he studies me.

"There is passion in you," he says in a low voice, walking in a slow, appraising circle around me like a shark testing the waters. "You will have to learn to release it. Seduce us. Become sensual. It is not a suggestion but a prerequisite," he says at my back, and I turn to face him.

He gazes back at me. "Do you understand my implication?"

I shake my head.

"Take. A. Lover," he says, and a blush storms up my face, the sweat of my body slicking to a boiling heat.

"Pish," Boel hisses, seeing the redhead's blush that I can't hide, regardless of my disguised appearance. "Do not be naïve. Each dancer has a catalyst." He gazes off at the other dancer, who pirouettes flawlessly. "That one will make an excellent living background."

*Non-frontline performer,* I translate.

The sun slants through the high glass of the auditorium windows, striking the mirrors they've installed like a ruthless weapon and backlighting Boel.

He looks slightly demonic as he stands there.

"But you . . ." He circles me again as he casually commands my rival: "Again," he says, spinning a finger in the air.

I can almost feel her sigh.

I turn with him; I don't want him at my back.

"You could be principal if you but released your passion." His eyes drill me. "Something has held it back and I feel it"— he puts a fist to his heart—"here."

I nod like I understand and he moves with his powerful grace against me so closely a sheet of paper could barely fit between us. I move to step back and he grabs my wrist.

"Dance with me—now."

I want to argue.

*I want to dance more.* He moves us out into the middle of the auditorium and swings me around, my eyes meeting his when I'm en pointe.

"You're tall," he says.

"I know," I say.

"Almost too tall."

I say nothing, moving against him, my eyes partially closed, and I imagine only the music. It is all and everything I can do to relax myself.

As it swells in the open we reach the crescendo, he grips my thighs to lift me and I let him.

I rise above his head and he whispers, "Convince me."

I slide down the front of Boel's body and he throws me away from him. I spin into the momentum and at the last moment he grips my fingertips and spins me back into his arms, where we end as the last note spins into the stale air of the auditorium.

"You will not quit today," he says.

"No," I respond, my leotard and tights soaked through, my feet throbbing inside my shoes.

"Tomorrow then." He drops my hands and walks away. As he passes the other dancer he barks, "Four o'clock."

She waits until he's out of sight, then flips him the bird.

"Did I sign up for this fucking torture?" she asks.

I give a slight smile. I'm so tired I don't know my own name. But I'm dancing. "Yes you did," I reply.

"How're your feet?" Then the girl sticks out her hand. "I'm Shelby."

We shake hands. "Jess. And they feel like they've been through a meat grinder."

Shelby laughs in sage agreement. "Did you look this dude up? Man . . . he's like the tyrant of ballet."

*Yeah, I did.*

"He likes you," she says, fishing.

"He's gay," I guess.

"Bi, baby," Shelby says, like I care.

I walk through the gym doors, spy a wooden bench and make a beeline for it. I can't wait to get my pointe shoes off. I sit down and Shelby does with a grateful sigh.

"Whatever," I say, unraveling my satin ribbons from one sweating ankle, slowly guiding my cramped foot out of the square toe box. I remove the wool that's been flattened from the pressure of my toes and anticipate the pins and needles to come.

My toes flood with circulating blood. My foot wakes up, grinding through the physical release of escaping its prison of satin.

"Ooh," Shelby croons, doing a mirror of my reaction. We toss our slippers in front of us and lean back on the unforgiving locker room bench. We sit quietly for a moment or two.

"What'd he say to ya?" Shelby asks, folding gum into her mouth as I unbraid my hair.

"That I need more passion when I dance . . ."

"Ooh . . . passion!" She laughs. Then she gives me a sharp look. "Did he say anything about me?"

"No," I lie.

"Huh," she huffs, then smiles, lifting a finger in the air. "Time for a de-skank."

I can't help it; I smile. My body is beaten but I'm happy.

I head back to my dorm room, my pointe shoes bundled and twisted in an automatic collision of satin and laces.

I keep to the lighted areas. I can't shake the feeling that someone is watching me. I know it's just a reaction to Brock the other day . . . and the news of some whack-job going after female students.

Nevertheless, an uneasy creepiness eats at the edges of me, and when I reach my room I'm happy to insert my key in the lock, jiggling it out before I close myself in my room.

*Just nerves,* I think, gathering my shower gear and heading back out to clean up.

This time, I use a completely different route to the showers. It's twice as long.

But safer.

# SIX

"Shut up!" Carlie says.

"No, really," I say, staring straight into her dark eyes, "he had me up against entrance D, and no"—my lips curl—"it doesn't stand for *dick*."

Carlie smirks.

"So operation Avoid Devin Castile?" she asks.

"Is so on," I say in agreement.

"What about Mitch?" She pauses, putting a finger to her pouty lips thoughtfully, nibbling on a long nail. "He's super cute . . ."

"How about super embarrassing?" I say, folding my clean ballet gear and putting it away in a small thrift-store dresser I bought with the little discretionary money I had. It has drawers that stick instead of slide. I jam the stuff in there and slam it with my palm and it closes. Sort of.

"Stop abusing your shit and listen up," Carlie says.

I grab my bio textbook and head for my door, the knob rattling as I jerk it open.

"That prick jock is still in your bio?"

I nod. "He's not sitting in front of Brad and me anymore though."

"That's good, that fucker . . . look what he did to you!"

The bruises have faded but my nerves haven't. I'm so going to be looking over my shoulder when I'm in class.

Sometimes when I'm not.

Brock has made me paranoid.

"Just report his brick-head ass," Carlie says.

*No, that'll get me even more attention.* "Nah." My eyes meet hers, then I shift them away. I've never been very good at containing my emotions. "Nothing happened . . . really."

Carlie mutters grumpily, "His dumb ass needs to be reported! You have marks!" Then she gives me a grin. "I like the way Castile did him up."

I give a vague smile; it was rather amazing. I shove my thoughts away. "It doesn't matter, as long as he keeps away from me . . ."

"And the biker dude doesn't piss him off again."

"Yeah, I think I'm gonna have to tell him," I say nervously.

"Tell someone, Jess. What makes you think that you can keep something like this to yourself?" Carlie's eyes become serious for once and I realize that a normal girl would have gone to campus security about Brock's threatening and physical behavior.

But I'm not a normal girl.

I'm the missing daughter of the South Dakota senator who

is running for president. My natural father is dead and my mother made her choice.

And it wasn't me.

I live under the constant threat of discovery. Dancing has become a selfish and stupid act on my part. I can't also go running to the authorities because some asshole has a hurt ego and bad manners.

And reminds me of Thad. I shudder at the memory.

I can't elaborate on my thoughts so I shrug at Carlie's logic and say offhandedly, "I'm just embarrassed about the whole thing; I don't want to spotlight it, Carlie."

She huffs. "Fine. But just because he's not hassling you and doesn't park his ass in front of you and Biker Dude anymore"—I smile at her nickname for Brad—"doesn't mean that he is done with harassing you . . . you feelin' me, girlfriend?" Her dark eyes capture mine and hold them prisoner.

I turn, giving her a wave behind my back. "I'll be careful, stop worrying . . ."

"I call bullshit!" she yells. Typical Carlie, having to have the last word. Her eyelids drop like bricks and she repeats in a low voice, "Shenanigan bullshit."

I can feel her stew behind me as I walk away without comment.

⁓

I'm almost safely to biology when I feel someone fall into step beside me, my mind already on the Punnett-square packet, which is finally complete. I startle a little and then flush deeply when I see that it's Mitch.

*Shit-damn-shit.* "Hey," he says softly.

"Hi," I say back, my embarrassment from a few days prior roaring back to dismal life again.

"Truce?" he asks, and I stop walking.

I roll my eyes up to his, his pale gaze filled with remorse. I look down again. "Listen." I roll my lip into my mouth nervously, then release it from my teeth. "I know it looked bad with Devin and me."

His brows rise.

"Okay, really bad," I say, then laugh, and he does too.

I shrug a little helplessly. "I didn't mean for that to happen. He took care of Brock and I was feeling . . ."

"Vulnerable?" he asks, his expression softening with a smile that makes the cleft in his chin flatten and disappear.

I nod. "I'm grateful to Devin but . . ."

"Not that grateful."

I laugh. "I can speak, you know," I say with a smirk.

He nods. "You sure can."

We stand there for a minute, his dark hair still damp from the shower, and I'm reminded of how sexy I thought he was, how safe Mitch Maverick is compared to Devin Castile.

I make a decision. Leaning forward, I rise to my tiptoes, my feet letting me know they are still sore, and give him a quick hug. "Thanks for understanding."

"Still on for dinner?" he asks, releasing me reluctantly, his fingers clinging like taffy to my body.

"Sure," I say as the next-period bell rings.

He takes my hand and pulls me close. I'm so sure he's going to kiss me but instead his words are cold water on my face.

"We're gonna talk about Brock and what happened, Jess."

*Right. Talking about Brock. Totally don't want to.* "Okay."

He hesitates a moment, wanting to do more, not sure if he should. Finally, he releases me and I walk into the class.

Devin would have kissed me. Whether or not I'd said yes.

That should scare me.

Instead, it does the opposite.

I've let the incident of violence between Brock and me simmer on the backburner. The more I tell myself I should keep it bottled up inside me, the more I feel the need to tell someone. Like a bottle uncapped for the first time, it needs to breathe. I've gone days with only Carlie knowing, which means Amber too, and now I feel compelled to include Brad. Anonymity used to be so easy, like breathing. Now I find it suffocates me in every way.

Brad's expression darkens with each word I lay at his feet.

When I'm done recounting the events of last week his hands clench into fists. "I'm gonna rip that fucker's head off and shit down his throat."

I get a visual of a headless Brock with Brad squatting and grunting out a growler. I contain myself with an effort.

"Ah, no!" I say, clutching the black leather of his jacket before he makes his way over to the circle of jocks who are gathered at the opposite end of the hall.

Brock's eyes meet Brad's and he gives a chin lift and a middle finger at Brad.

"That prick," Brad says, stepping forward.

"No, Brad," I say, then add, "He scares me, he'll hurt me."

That stops Brad. I give him the biggest eyes I have and he stares down at my face.

"He can't hurt you if his face is broken," Brad says, grinding the words out, and I gulp.

"True," I say slowly, "but he's got friends and I don't want him to notice me." I look at him significantly, then say, "More."

Brad stands there and silently seethes, scanning the group of six guys. "He's a huge pussy to lay his hands on you." He looks at them, then gives me his dark eyes. "I hear shit about him."

*I don't want to know.* "What?" I ask.

"Just guy-posturing bullshit."

I wait, folding my arms, and he sighs, raking a hand through his longish hair.

"Y'know, date-rape shit."

*That is a real rape,* I think, *there's no line between rape that happens on a date, it's not predicated on location.*

My heart stutters and I think of Thad. As my heart thumps at my own dump of memories I tell myself that his hands on me in the hallways of my former home, the sly pinching gropes and looks that held dark promise can't hurt me here.

I think of Faith; they're hopelessly intertwined in the bank of my memories. She held me up, affirmed me through the worst of his threats. When Faith first called him on his behavior and I finally had a witness, she'd done two things: made him aware, and put his focus on me with even more intent. I realize now that no one could have won. Thad had tried his threats with Faith and she had been unmoved. That's when he'd decided. He knew that she would never be cowed by him, intimidated. Thad used the solution that made the most sense to him. A final one.

"Are you okay?" Brad asks, and his voice comes to me through a tunnel, his brow furrowing between his eyes.

"Yeah," I respond. "Fine."

"You don't look fine," Brad says doubtfully. "You look like you've seen a ghost."

*Or one walked over my grave,* I think as memory recall eats at the edges of my brain.

"I'll take it from here, Gunner," a voice like gravel states.

*Oh shit, it's Castile.* My insides flutter, the butterflies loose and whirling with just the sound of his voice.

Brad's eyes narrow; mine go to where Brock is standing. When I see that he's gone, oxygen fills my lungs.

No one is scarier than Thad. I survived him. I can survive anything.

I look at Devin and he's wearing his usual leather, a crisp, white beefy tee stretched to bursting over the muscles of his chest, the steel-reinforced black boots boosting his height to over six foot four, like he needs it.

He makes Brad look small, and that's saying something.

"You know Castile?" Brad asks me.

I nod. *Don't ask,* my face begs.

Brad watches me. "Jess here says she knows you, dude . . . but acts like she doesn't want to, if you dig my meaning."

Devin turns to Brad and they position themselves in a subtle square-off.

I put my hand on Brad's arm, the leather giving underneath my touch. "It's okay, Brad. He helped, okay?"

Of course, only Devin and I know how much he "helped." To his credit, his face remains stoically neutral.

Brad's shoulders relax.

"Treat her right, Castile," Brad says, warning him.

"I'll treat her how she wants to be treated," he says as he turns those blazing brown eyes on mine, "won't I?"

"Yes," I breathe, knowing it's true. Castile is like an unmovable force. A hurricane on its own course, its destination known only to it. The trajectory likely to change at any time.

Taking anything or anyone in its path.

As I look into those dark eyes, I know I am in the eye of the storm that is Devin Castile.

~

Devin has his hands jammed into his pockets but as we come to the first door he punches it open ahead of me. I pass through, the noise reverberating in the hall filled with students filing in opposite directions.

He is moody and quiet and I am just . . . quiet.

Operation Avoid Castile is a dismal failure. He obviously isn't gunning for my success.

"I can't date you," I blurt into the noisy atmosphere.

"Who said I wanted that?" he growls.

I stop and turn to him, the students flowing on opposite sides of our bodies like the Red Sea parting.

"What?" I ask, feeling suddenly thick and stupid, like I'm swimming through mud. Or quicksand.

Then he blows me away with his next phrase.

"What about just fucking?" he asks.

I'm stunned. When I finally recover, I shake my head. "I can't believe you just said that here." *I can't believe he said it at all.*

But the more I think about it, the more it makes a sort of crass sense. But not for the reasons he's thinking.

Castile is thinking we can just quench this fire between us.

I'm thinking I can avoid the emotional entanglement if he doesn't care about me. If he just cares about sex, there'll be no probing questions.

No finding out my real identity.

I walk like I'm in a stupor and he prowls after me, saying nothing.

I'm pissed that he's read everything so well. That he's sussed out what my body wants even if I haven't admitted it to myself.

The prick.

A flush rises to the surface of my skin with what I know I want to do with him.

I stop outside my physics class and I can feel his heated presence behind me.

Large hands turn me to face him. Castile's eyes search my face.

"I see yes," he states. His eyes brook no argument; yet paradoxically they implore me to give permission.

"Yes," I say.

"Yes *what*, Jess?" he asks, barely above a whisper, his hands on either side of my head, the hallway ours, the students already cocooned in a class I should be in.

But I'm not; I'm out in the hall with a dangerous man.

"To fucking," I say, and can't believe I've said the words out loud.

"Yes . . . to fucking," he repeats, and jerks me to him, crushing my mouth with his, forcing my lips open for his tongue, and I let him, my core moistening with heat, and I'm suddenly lost.

In the hall of a faraway school, I toy with the danger of exposure because I weep for Castile's touch.

I pull away, half staggering, my hand touching my swollen lips, and he gives a cocky grin. "Tasty," he says.

"I'm dating Mitch," I say, and a flash of something crosses his face and is gone before I can read the emotion. It almost comes to me but his words shatter the epiphany before I can latch on to it.

"I don't share," he says, warning me, and moves toward me again, his expression darkening as my eyes latch on to his sensuous mouth.

"Fine," I say reflexively.

"Don't fuck him," Castile orders.

We stare at each other. I know when a treacherous game has begun.

"I don't want him to know . . . ," I say in a shaky voice, a fine tremble in my hands as I push escaped wisps of hair behind my ears.

His mouth turns up at the corners. "Don't worry, Jess. My cock's for the taking, your pussy is not." His coarse language should derail me. My need for blending in should come first. My latent fear of males should kick in for self-preservation's sake. I wait for logic to assert itself. With each second that ticks by, Devin's smile widens. Finally, he grins.

I sigh, utterly disgusted with myself.

Utterly decided.

I want Devin Castile and have agreed to his terms. He just doesn't know why.

A decision fueled by lust, secured by my desire for anonymity. Perfect.

I watch him walk off, a mountain of lethal tattooed muscle: purposeful, intense, sexual.

And soon to consume me.

$\sim$

"Okay," Carlie says, whipping her curly hair over her shoulder and turning on her signal. She gives a glance to the right and then the left. When the coast is clear, she inches out into traffic. "So you've finally decided to join us sluts . . . awesome," she says, keeping her eyes on the road.

I bark out a laugh. "Not really," I say, trying to defend the indefensible.

"Oh yes. Fucking-A really, Jess." She shifts her gaze off the road and pegs me with serious eyes.

I become quiet.

"You've been with what? Two guys?"

I put two fingers in the air.

She nods, her eyes straying to the slick pavement, the light drizzle that falls slicking the road with a dangerous mixture like butter on a griddle. The oncoming headlights pierce the dark interior of the car as I put my knees slightly underneath me, sweeping my bent legs until my high heels touch the door, and face Carlie.

"And," she drawls, "it's been two years. Sounds like the curse of the twos."

I smile in the gloom. Carlie has a way of phrasing things.

"Let's hope he doesn't have a two-inch dick," she says, stabbing the accelerator through a hole in traffic.

I gasp, grabbing the oh-shit handle in the Jeep. "Come on!"

"Coming . . . ," she says, and winks.

"God, you're so bad," I say.

We're silent for a minute, pulling up to Amber's house. She's appropriated her parents' basement and there's a door with a low porch light attached, illuminating steep concrete stairs to what she lovingly refers to as "the dungeon."

"Did you text her?"

"As we speak . . . ," Carlie says, blowing a spiral curl out of her vision as she furiously texts Amber with her nails.

I turn at the waist to face Carlie.

"There!" She stabs the send button and looks at me. "What?"

"Don't tell Amber."

"She's gonna think you're doin' both of them."

*Ugh. Terrible.* "Tell her I'm a player."

"You're not. You're a ballerina posing as a student." Carlie's brows arch.

I smile; that's a fair assessment. "I don't have to date just one guy."

"True," Carlie says in a droll way, studying perfectly good sparkly acrylic nail tips.

"I hear a *but* . . ."

"You haven't dated anyone since you came here." Her eyes meet mine. "And then there's the mysterious transfer hunk-o-love with a dark reputation, Devin Castile."

*I can see why his reputation is dark.* "Wait, isn't Mitch new too?" I know Carlie has the Guy Roster memorized.

She nods. "He's a hybrid, did his first two years at a community college, then transferred here." Carlie shrugs. "Don't know why . . . ," she starts to say, then gives a furious flap at Amber as she comes up the the subterranean steps of the dungeon, her high heels clacking on the wet sidewalk that leads to the curb where Carlie's car idles.

She troops over to the car and opens the back passenger door, sliding in with a sigh.

"I hate this shitty weather!" Amber fumes. "Effing November drizzle!"

I turn to face forward.

"IDs, girls?" Carlie asks, turning the car back on.

We wave ours like flags.

Of course I have ID. For two different names. I emptied my trust fund to make it happen. With enough money, anything is obtainable.

We pull up to Skoochie's. The nondescript, flat-roofed

building has crap parking but is high on my list of places to be anonymous: it's dark, it's primal, the bouncers skim fake IDs and there's lots of dancing.

Perfect.

We don't bother to lock the door on the car; Carlie always says, *If they want it, let them have it.* It hardly runs.

There's already a line and I go to the back with the rest of the made-up crowd of twentysomethings.

"Holy shit," Amber breathes.

I look where she's pointing and my stomach drops.

The bouncer is Devin Castile.

Of course.

So much for anonymity.

# SEVEN

~

*I* was thinking I'd get a girls' night out. No. Such. Luck. Those dark eyes scan the crowd. They skid to a stop and shift back to me.

My breath stops as Devin Castile drives his eyes down my body like a freight train. Just that searing appraisal causes heat to bloom, the moistening of my panties a success, that dull ache revisiting me. Then those restless eyes move on. He's obviously in work mode. Some clearly underage guys try to sidle past him and the other bouncer. He gives them the look. They aren't getting in. I can tell; I'm sure everyone else can too. But the asshat is a slow learner.

He gets cocky and gets tossed four feet away by a casual fist in his shirt courtesy of Devin.

I watch as muscles bunch and spring taut during the maneuver, like he's done it a million times. Maybe he has.

Carlie watches the testosterone purge and looks at me, brow

arched. "Huh, seems like Castile's a versatile guy." She laughs, then shushes herself in a hurry.

"Hey, he's coming this way, Jess . . . ," Amber says in awe, like the president is coming for tea. Of course, Amber is going on old information. She doesn't know I've sold my soul to the devil.

*Only sex, only sex, only sex,* I sing to myself like the tuneless mantra it is.

Devin is suddenly there, looking down at me, the streetlight illuminating the side of his face: the square jaw, his eyes like black jewels. He says nothing for a heartbeat, then, "Hi."

My heart races. "Hi," I say, feigning relaxation and losing by a mile. He seems to pick up on my discomfort and gives me a break, staying in the role of casual acquaintance instead of almost-sex-commando and breaks our stare. He turns to Carlie. "Hey," he says, and she gives him a coy smile back. He chin-dips at Amber and she twitters at the minute attention.

"Hi, Devin," Carlie says, and a flustered Amber gives a little rippling wave of her scarlet nails.

His brows rise. "Do I know you?" He's addressing Carlie. I die, silently hoping that she doesn't give away that I've told all.

"Castile!" A male voice raises like a flag of noise from the entrance. Devin stiffens but lifts a hand. Like anyone can't see where he is because of his height.

"I'm ballerina girl's bestie, Castile," Carlie says like he's dim-witted.

A frown forms on Castile's face as the faceless male voice rises for a second time, irritation flashing over his face. "Just a sec!" Devin shouts back.

His eyes meet mine. "I know she dances. Is that what

defines Jess?" he asks Carlie in a soft voice. Of course he knows I dance. *He* was the one silently studying me at the tryouts. It was unforgettable.

It's Carlie's turn to frown.

She looks at me and I give a small shrug. I'm not entirely sure what he's asking.

"She . . . I don't know. Jess dances," she says, as confused as I am.

The crowd grows restless and just as I think Devin is probing for something I don't want to give, that male voice shouts out again.

But the tone has changed.

"A little help!" Nameless bellows.

Castile's head swivels toward the sound and he issues a low hiss of annoyance.

I gasp when I see who it is that the other bouncer is having a hard time containing.

Brock.

Devin gives me a loaded glance, then jogs over to his fellow bouncer, and seeing that Brock is giving as good as he's getting, Devin wades into the flashing fists and meaty smacks of a fight in full throttle. I can't believe that Brock is here, that Castile is a bouncer here at Skoochie's in the seediest part of Seattle.

As if on dreadful cue, I hear a familiar voice and realize that everything has just ratcheted up into a special kind of complicated.

"Hey, Jess," Mitch says.

I turn and there he is, looking good enough to eat. The one I will be eating is busy pounding Brock's face in.

*Oh good Lord.*

Mitch gazes at the two bouncers restraining Brock, and then Brock's fleet of loser friends stomp in and the tide turns against the bouncers.

Suddenly, it's two bouncers against five college athletes who are soaked in booze and driven by a lack of inhibition.

I don't think; I run over to Devin, the man who's an enigma to me, and watch as two of Brock's friends hold him, the other two beating the other bouncer. I skid to a stop, my spiky heels making a clatter as I break through the noisy crowd, everyone straining to watch the bouncers get their asses kicked, getting into the club forgotten for the show of blood and fists.

"Do something!" I yell to Mitch.

But Mitch shakes his head. "Castile can take care of himself," he says with a sarcastic snort.

I know I'm just a girl. I know that Devin wants to screw me, not love me.

Those are the glaring and unforgiving facts.

It doesn't seem to matter. Sometimes emotion reigns supreme and all I can think of is getting in there and distracting them long enough for Devin to break free as my soon-to-be-boyfriend stands and watches the unfairness unravel.

I can't.

Carlie anticipates me somehow and shrieks as I move forward, "Jess, no!"

Mitch is completely surprised by my next move and too far away to stop what happens next. He's late holding me back and I sweep in with my purse, a small suitcase, and bash the beater on the back of the head. He staggers a little at the blow and it's enough.

I'll never know if it's because of my lame distraction, but it seems like Devin has already freed one arm, and that in combination with my interference is all it takes.

"Jess!" I hear Mitch yell, and as the beater turns, he sees the purse spilled on the wet pavement and his eyes meet mine for a suspended moment. Then the knowledge that I'm a woman fills his eyes seconds before he backhands me.

It looks great in the movies, as the heroine who is victimized falls gracefully to the ground in a sexy tumble.

The reality was oh so different. "No!" I hear Castile roar as I fall in an unladylike sprawl on my ass, my skirt hiked up to my thighs, a sliver of the crotch of my panties on display for the world to see.

I'm hurt and humiliated as I watch two things happen simultaneously: Mitch and the girls run to my position on the ground as Devin Castile, with apparently renewed vigor, plows through the jocks, making his way like a human tornado to me.

I bat Mitch's hand away; I'm pissed and I don't know why.

I was the only one who wanted to do the right thing apparently. I can feel the moisture from the ground seeping into the back of my skirt as Devin reaches me a fraction of a second after Mitch.

Behind him one of the jocks falls like an unbalanced bowling pin, landing with a sickening thud behind him, the abuse of his face from the fists that hang by Devin's sides looking like the result of a meat plow that visited and stayed awhile.

"Jess," Castile says in a low voice as Mitch reaches for my hand. My eyes widen and I sit there on the ground, my cheek throbbing from the hit by one of Brock's friends. The guy who wants to be my boyfriend gives me a hand and the man I want inside me says my name without a trace of indifference. The caliber of emotion I hear in that one word says more than any endearment could.

Devin looks at the hand Mitch offers me and says, "Fuck off, Maverick. A day fucking late and a buttload of cash short, pal."

Mitch hauls me up anyway and I fight a shooting pain in my head as the suddenness of the motion threatens me with vertigo.

The crowd has dispersed now that the fight has ended and a third bouncer is cautiously letting in the handpicked crowd, his eyes wary and watchful.

While five guys and the other bouncer groan and writhe on the wet ground in various stages of consciousness.

"You listen to me, Castile," Mitch says with barely contained anger, "why is it that every time you're around, Jess is threatened?" He gives Castile a direct look.

Carlie puts a hand on my arm and leans her head into my shoulder, whispering, "You dumbshit."

I nod soundlessly; I couldn't agree more. It was a stupid move, and I knew better, but somehow, that reactive nature of mine wouldn't stay still.

Devin doesn't refute Mitch's words. Instead, he just folds his muscular arms across a vintage T-shirt that reads, *Go ahead, make my day.* Beside the slogan, there is a fine splatter of blood like an artist threw paint at his chest. I run my eyes over his body, taking in the shredded skin of his knuckles, the cut above his eye that slowly oozes blood but is trying to close as I watch.

Finally, my gaze lands on his beautiful, full lips. Lips that have crushed mine with a velvet intensity. I see the marring split on his lower lip and want to suck on it and make it better.

I gulp and his nostrils flare at the scorching look I give him.

Carlie looks between the two of us, seeing the potential for an unraveling moment of epic proportions.

Mitch pulls on my arm. "Let's go, Jess."

Devin steps forward, moving as if to touch me, and I shy away. I'm so confused. I offered myself up for the slaughter when he was attacked, like I could do anything. I don't even know what possessed me to do it. Then Mitch shows up and I can't reason or respond for myself. Pathetic.

We made plans, Devin and I, and they didn't include the world knowing. I plead with my eyes for him not to make Mitch the wiser. For him to keep the arrangement a secret.

There is a pregnant pause that feels like the Grand Canyon opening up underneath us.

I see his frustration, his indecision . . . as his hand drops and Mitch hauls me away, a stunned Amber and a puzzled Carlie falling in our wake.

I glance back and Castile is standing there watching us go, having never made a rebuttal to Mitch's accusation that he is a danger magnet to me.

It's true.

But not for the reasons Mitch thinks.

Castile mouths a word at me right before I'm ushered into that vintage Camaro of Mitch's.

It looks like *thanks*.

~

Carlie's pissed, tapping her high heel. "Okay, she's not some baby, I can take her back to the dorms, Mitch," she says.

Mitch gathers me against him and asks softly, "Are you okay?"

Tears threaten and I nod against his broad chest. "Yeah, I'm okay."

I turn my face to the side that's not hurting and Carlie sees my expression and huffs out an exasperated sigh. "Why, Jess?"

Amber pipes up. "Yeah, I mean, there's like a hundred and one guys that could have gone to the ground for Castile but you, what . . . bash the guy over the head with your Guess purse?" Amber clucks out that last with a laugh and I can't find the humor no matter how hard I look.

"Yeah," I say. Mitch tilts my chin up, examining my cheek.

"That's going to bruise," he says, angry.

I shrug. "He helped me," I say defensively, referencing the Brock incident.

Mitch shrugs. "Him jamming his tongue down your throat is not helping, Jess."

I blush to the roots of my hair and am thrilled that it's night and my redhead's complexion doesn't give me away.

"Are you talking about the Brock Episode, Jess?" Amber inquires.

I nod.

Carlie throws her hands up in the air. "Fine, go with La Hunk, but not out past one!"

Mitch raises a brow.

"She might look like she can kick people's ass using her purse like a weapon and all, but Jess . . . Jess needs protecting," Carlie says, like she doesn't want to.

I don't. I'm used to not having any protection. I lived that life. Carlie has me dead wrong.

Dead.

I open my mouth to argue that and Mitch answers, "I know, I'll take care of her."

I give up, giving Carlie a tight hug instead. "I'm sorry I screwed our girls' night," I say.

"It's okay, purse bludgeoner." She smooths the wisps of my hair behind my ear and it feels eerily like what my mom used to do before becoming Senator MacLeod's wife. A life so distant and soft in my memory it hurts to recall it.

I gulp back the lump in my throat and she leans away, her eyes searching my face, hesitating over the tenderness of my cheek. "Are ya sure, Jess?" she asks in a very un-Carlie-like voice, giving me an out if I want it.

"Yes," I say, shoving as much of a resolute note into the affirmative as I can.

"Okay," she says, and loops her arm through Amber's. "Onward and upward."

I crack a grin and grimace. It hurts but I hold the expression in place because it's genuine and Carlie needs to see it so she can have fun.

She does and grins back. I give her a subtle nod and she walks off to the club again, leaving me with Mitch.

We stand awkwardly for a moment at ten o'clock on a

Friday night, a second date not even under our belt, and I am about ready to let him go.

The relationship farce suddenly seems insane: I can't do it, it won't go anywhere, Castile says I can't sleep with him.

*Why am I listening to Devin Castile?* I hear his words in my mind: *I don't share.*

I shiver. I'm not sure why and I'm not interested in analyzing it.

Mitch watches whatever emotions wash over my face in the gloom of the night.

"How about that dinner date?" he asks, and I hang on the edge of the chasm of jumping or fleeing. Now is the time to come clean, to tell him that I think I just want to be friends . . . that I'm conflicted.

*What an understatement.*

Mitch waits and I see the fine muscles in his forearms ripple as he shoves his hands in his front jean pockets, flipping dark hair back out of his eyes, their paleness in sharp contrast to the blackness that surrounds us.

Instead of doing what I should, I do what I want, grabbing on to more than mere existence while I can.

"Okay," I say, and exhale with relief. At least I've made a decision.

Not the right one, but I'm sticking to it.

His smile flashes in the night and he holds out his large hand. I slip mine inside his and he pulls me to him, placing a gentle peck on my lips. I sigh.

Mitch is safe.

# EIGHT

⁓

*He* takes me to an all-night diner; I'm too far gone emotionally to even notice the name.

I like the way Mitch touches me. His hand warms the small
of my back as we enter the eatery, very near Pike Place Market,
still so alive even at this hour, and he lets me slide into the
booth ahead of him, hesitates, then finally decides to sit opposite me.

Safe.

The waitress hovers at Mitch's elbow, dismissing me with
my scraped face and wet ass. I'm sure I look awful. I try to muster up the proper embarrassment but can't do it.

In fact . . . "Why don't you order some coffee for me, I'm
going to hit the bathroom." I rise gracefully; over a decade of
ballet doesn't desert me just because I've had a rough night and
I'm wearing heels. Boel would be proud.

Mitch smiles and nods, turning his attention to—*Doris,* the crooked name tag reads on her crisp uniform, in sharp contrast to her badly dyed red hair, which is fading to pink, as all red dye jobs eventually do.

I float to the bathroom in a surreal fog, so wrapped up in what happened I could be blown over by a feather.

I open the door and it slams back, making me jump at the noise. I level a dirty look at it, heave my purse on top of the vanity's only dry spot and get a look at the damage.

It looks worse than it feels. Half my face is an angry red with a welt that appears like a raised comma on my cheekbone, my fair skin making it stand out like a zebra stripe. The area is swollen and raw. It makes me angry all over again at the prick who hit me.

Of course, I did wallop him over his head with my handbag. I dig deeply in my purse for a makeup wipe. I take off everything, carefully cleaning the wound, wincing as I go over the worst of it. Then I peer closer, prepping to apply a new round of mascara, and notice the worst thing ever.

One of my blue contacts popped out in the melee and a green eye blazes out of my fair complexion, accentuated by the injury, red intensifying the green.

Kinda like Xmas.

I give a shaky laugh at my dumb internal dialogue and turn away, taking down my hair from its normal loose messy bun. The curls spin out in soft rolling spirals, feathering at my waist. I can use my hair like a curtain and hope it'll distract from my eye color discrepancy.

Maybe Mitch won't notice.

Maybe I can claim vanity. I mean . . . plenty of girls want a different eye color.

It's a little bit on the stretchy side of the truth considering how low-maintenance I am in general. How could I convince anyone that I care about eye color when my entire makeup routine consists of moisturizer, mascara and lip gloss?

I roll my unglossed lip into my mouth and bite down gently, nibbling with nervousness. Finally, I realize I need to get back there or Mitch'll wonder if I died.

I walk back to the table and he turns, watching my approach.

It was a good idea about the hair. He can't get past it long enough to notice my eye color. It occurs to me that he's never seen it down.

I let the relief wash over me as I slide into the bench seat opposite him and Doris sets a steaming cup of coffee in front of me. Instantly, I wrap my fingers around the hot cup and sigh in pleasure. Just having the coffee in my hands makes the events of the night seem a tiny bit more bearable, normal.

Mitch looks down at his own cup and I notice his tapered fingers overlap. Long fingers, artist's fingers.

He watches me watching him, then asks me the question I'm dreading: "What's with you and Castile, Jess?" His eyes search mine and I make a stab at honesty.

"I don't know . . . exactly," I say, back to nibbling my lip again.

He rakes a hand through his hair, and I'm reminded of the shadow on Devin's head and shake away the memory like unwanted mist.

Mitch leans forward, the light from the street shadowing his pale gray eyes perfectly, deepening them to a storm. "Because . . . I think we have something here. I think I can give you what you need."

My heart begins to beat hard in my chest at his words, my mouth going dry. "What is that?" I croak.

He takes my hand in his, gently turning it over, and I watch him raise it to his mouth and put a single, heated kiss on the underside of my wrist. I tingle where he touches and hold in a shiver. It isn't the demolishing sexual intensity I got a taste of with Devin, but it's a nice enough distraction and I'm not immune.

"Me," he says. Then, after an exaggerated pause, he says, "All of me."

The revelation is too much; it feels like an elephant has landed on my chest.

He watches my face and gives a little lift of his lips. "Have I lost you to Devin Castile?" he asks quietly, his probing gaze never leaving mine.

"I'm not a prize," I say, "something to be won or . . . whatever." I hold my hands out to the sides. "I'm just a girl who likes a guy."

"Two guys," he says, probing with uncanny accuracy.

"Actually . . . yes," I say.

*I don't share.*

"May the best man win, then, Jess." He leans back, studying me.

"What?" I ask, confused for the second time in two hours. "I mean . . ." I pause, then continue with hesitation. "Why me?

There's a million girls more special, prettier . . . with bigger boobs," I say with a smile to lighten the heavy conversation.

Mitch inclines his head and the cleft in his chin deepens with the shadows as he glances through the bay window, then back at me. "True on one count . . ." I briefly wonder which one but he goes on before I have a chance to consider which inadequacy he's noticed. "However, that you'd ask is the very reason why you're so attractive . . ." He continues to stare at me, then adds a last word, "Sexy."

"Thank you . . . I think."

"You're welcome, Jess Mackey with one green eye."

My stomach drops; he's noticed all right. I'm in deep shit.

I race through a response and he holds up his hand. "I don't need to know why you'd cover up those eyes." Then he winks. "It just deepens the mystery."

"What mystery?" I whisper, wiping my suddenly damp hands on my even damper hem.

"The mystery that is you, Jess."

I yawn behind my hand and pick up the mechanical pencil again, taking studious notes in my own version of shorthand, while Brad has his legs kicked out in front of him, huge boots crossed at the ankles, as he taps out a tune on the desk only he hears.

"Shush . . . ," I say, warning him that he'll get the wrong attention, which seems to be the trend with Brad.

Brad winks and shoots me with a finger pistol. My curtain

of hair falls away from my face and I know when he sees the bruise that marks me.

Brad sits straight up in the desk and says in a furious whisper, "What. The. Fuck . . . is that?"

Automatically my hand goes to the tender lump that I iced all weekend. The swelling is gone but a light bruise and a glaring abrasion remain.

"Uh . . . ," I say lamely. "Wrong place at the wrong time?"

"Shush . . . ," the girl with braces in front of us says. Brock's replacement. As a matter of fact, I can feel his malignant presence like a walking tumor from across the room, his eyes on me.

"Turn around," Brad snaps.

"Fine!" she hisses back at him, flinging her back against the seat with an exaggerated huff.

I smile a little; she is almost worse than Brock was. How can it be in a class of three hundred souls that we get stuck with the biggest butts in the entire group? Murphy's Law is how. If it can happen, it will definitely happen to me. My smile widens and Brad frowns.

"Uh-uh, dancing girl. Tell me. Tell big Brad, baby."

I giggle; I can't help it. Prissy in front of us stiffens, giving me a peripheral glare.

I tell him. Brad's face is a study in comedy, his brows having a life of their own: popping to his hairline, then descending like a falling wall on his brow, only to rise again.

When I finish, having utterly missed the entire lecture on the delightful Punnett square, he crosses his arms in thought, his leather making a crinkling sound, not saying a word.

Class ends and I stand, stretching as the small bones of my

back pop at the motion. Brad watches me as I search for Brock and his cadre of pals. They give me a look and the one who belted me tips an imaginary hat in my direction.

"Is that the cocksucker who decked you?" Brad asks, already moving forward.

"No," I implore.

"Yes," he says, ignoring me while he moves too fast for me to stop him.

*Like I could,* I think, doing an internal eye-roll.

The jocks see the wall of black leather moving toward them and they stop, their eyes going first to him, then to me.

I shrink back into myself; I've never wished to be anywhere else as badly as I do right now.

That's not true; there is one incident I wish I could erase. I shut my eyes tightly, wishing myself away. When I open them, I'm still there.

"Brock." Brad says his name like a swear word.

The one who hit me looks at me but speaks to Brad: "Gunner."

"You the chick beater?" Brad asks him, his eyes all for the abuser.

"I don't hit girls who don't deserve it," he says sullenly, his beady gaze lingering on me as he evades the question.

"No girl deserves it, dickless," Brad declares. I can tell he's warming to his subject, subtly moving his body to square off with the other guy.

"You know what your problem is, Gunner?" Brock interjects congenially.

We wait and I know it's going to be bad and I move backward, finally wise to the potential for violence.

"You don't recognize what this is about." His eyes lock with Brad's. "Women are good for bagging and making sandwiches. That is it. The sooner you realize that basic principle, the less angry you'll be that the rest of us guys already have a handle on it," Brock says with classic stupidity.

Brad's hand pops out like a flesh torpedo, snapping Brock's head back, his face still showing marks from where Devin worked him over two days prior.

*I know I'll have his full attention now, a guaranteed spot,* I think with miserable finality.

"Leave"—thwack, crunch—"Jess Mackey alone." Brock crumples from the beating . . . I'm beginning to think he likes it. Kinda like a pastime or ill-considered hobby. Of the no-talent variety.

The guy who backhanded me moves in and Brad swings a well-placed boot and takes out his knee. The one he uses for football or some other full-contact sport will be out of commission for a while.

Two hundred thirty pounds drop like a sack of potatoes, and his two buddies come in to finish Brad, but he isn't done. He sweeps his arm out and swats the closest jerk. The guy wails, grabbing his ear.

"You can sing that tune all day long, ass jack," Brad says in a conversational tone, reversing the dis, keeping up his jabs and swipes.

Then campus security comes and pulls everyone apart. The two who are standing.

Brock isn't.

He's lying on the ground. Staring at me with hate so

apparent I can taste it. I step backward from that look and straight into the chest of Devin Castile.

Strong fingers curl around my shoulders and my nose fills with the smell of Devin: male, leather, fresh air and some undertone of whatever musky soap he uses. His scent is my drug of choice.

I stay against Castile. "I'm sorry," I say to Brad as he's dragged away.

"You're gonna be," Brock says in a low promise from the ground.

Castile comes around the side of me and squats down next to Brock. "Touch her again and you'll deal with me. And it'll be final, douche."

He straightens and gives a nod of acknowledgment to the campus police, who take the remaining four away.

"Gunner's a good sort," Devin says, his eyes watching until they disappear out of sight.

"Do you know them?" I ask, my eyes following the security guards, thinking about his nod at them. It looks like more than a greeting.

Devin nods, his face shutting down with my question. "Yeah, I work a part-time gig for campus security."

I don't say anything, hoping Brad will be okay. Instead I allow Castile to herd me to a dim corner where the eyes of the student body aren't staring at us. He moves in close, uncomfortably close. "I wanted to kick Maverick's ass for touching you." He moves his hand against my hair, palming it tightly against my skull.

I make a guttural sound low in my throat and his eyes move

to my mouth. "Don't make noises that make me want to take you right against the wall, Jess."

My eyes widen and he smiles his amusement at my taking him so literally. But there's that small part of me that knows he's serious. The bulge against my pelvic region is a real convincer.

"I—"

"Shush . . . ," Devin says, giving me a kiss as gentle as his last one was brutal, and I fall into it. Brad and Brock's entanglement is forgotten, and Mitch and my anonymity are distant concerns as Castile takes my lips, sipping at them like a fine cognac that he never wants to break contact with.

Finally, he leaves me against the wall, flushed and dazed; my backpack has slid down and leans cockeyed against the wall. The room is deserted of everyone but us.

Again.

"We're terrible together," I say, meeting his eyes, the savage truth hanging between us like an unmovable weight.

"It's not about true love, Jess." I see the conviction in his eyes and it is equal parts horrible and a comfort. I don't want a relationship, I want this burning ache to abate. The fire for him to subside.

I answer even though it's not required, jerking my backpack up off the ground as I begin to walk away. "If it were love then it would be a terrible love."

I don't wait for his response.

I swing and lunge, drops of sweat beading and flinging off my body like wet gems of punishment, the auditorium a ribboned blur of mixed colors, purple and gold becoming swimmingly gray. School colors morphing as I execute faster and faster pirouettes.

Finally, Instructor Boel claps. "Stop!"

His hands pegged on his hips, he stalks over to me and Shelby, on the warpath; at any moment I expect a Native American headdress to spring from his head.

"What. Is. This?" he asks, and his skin broils with color, his finger pointing to my face.

For a heartbeat I have no idea what he's talking about, then I remember the bruise. I fight touching it with an effort as I think of how nice it will be to have people stop asking me *what happened.*

Although how I used the purse-cum-weapon makes for a good story. Brock's group is not popular, so it's been well received.

I'm pretty sure that Brock's recounting would be quite a bit different.

Shelby waits as I tell my ballet instructor what happened. Of course, it sounds childish and foolish when I hear myself tell him. I put my hand on my sweaty hip; one foot goes up en pointe and I swivel it as I elaborate.

"We do not thwack people with accessories," he commands, adding, "You are a dancer, not a thug."

I flush, embarrassed. "Yes, Instructor Boel."

He studies me until I cast my eyes to the floor. "Do you wish to dance?"

I snap my eyes back to his. "More than anything."

"Then prove it by curtailing this ruffian behavior."

Shelby walks away, chancing a sympathetic glance at me.

I move to follow Shelby. "Wait, Miss Mackey," Boel says, grabbing my arm.

I stop.

"Have you thought about my comments?"

*Which ones?*

I watch his facial expression and I instantly know.

"Yes," I answer.

"Good," he says, then adds, "I await the passion that is absent in your dancing."

He releases me and I step away, gathering my sweater, and start walking, so sore and tired I want to sleep on the hard gym floor.

"Miss Mackey?"

I reluctantly turn.

"No more misbehavior, understood?"

I nod, wondering why he doesn't worry about the harm that befell me.

Right now it feels like I'm floating in a pool of anonymity of my own making. I don't like it anymore.

It feels like drowning.

# NINE

The state-of-the-art campus center is packed as per usual. Students are doing everything from studying to hanging to snacking. I take my seat and wait for Carlie and Amber. We'll pretend to study while actually getting in some much-needed girl time.

After all, our time was cut short by the episode outside of Skoochie's. That wonderful bit of history was still following me around almost a week later. Now it's the weekend all over again and I have two sets of smoldering looks following me.

Carlie saunters over, slinging her almost-thirty-pound backpack on the long cafeteria-style table.

"Hiya," she says, plopping down beside me.

"Hi," I reply.

Amber joins us and plops down, sans backpack. "Hey."

I arch a brow. "Where's your books?"

She tears the wrapper off a lollipop and jams it inside her mouth, sucking obscenely on it while not answering.

"Eeew," Carlie says.

I roll my eyes. "Like you think that's gross?" I say. "You're probably taking notes!" I laugh and Carlie scowls, muttering, "True."

Her scowl is phony and she breaks into a smile when I give her a disbelieving look.

"I'm supervising today," Amber says, sucking and slurping the bright green sour-apple knob, her tongue turning an alarming shade of green.

"So tell us about the beat-down outside bio," she says.

I hesitate; it's starting to sound like a soap opera, but I give her the condensed version, *Reader's Digest* style.

"So . . . you've got what? Two guys and two something elses?" Amber asks with a puzzled expression.

"It's like the twelve days of Christmas with a partridge in a pear tree," Carlie quips.

I shake my head with a nervous laugh. "No, it's *so* not like that."

Amber tears the sucker out of her mouth, swinging it like a prop. "What is it then?"

"Okay, so . . . Brock's a dick," I say, and the girls nod.

Carlie says slowly, "Clearly."

I sigh, the sounds of the busy study area swallowing our conversation. They remain unconvinced but I plow ahead, wanting them to see it my way, if possible. "Brad's my friend . . ."

"No way, girlfriend, he digs your cute dancing ass," Amber

states with absolute faith, her lips puckered in a distracting way around the green globe of the lollipop.

I shake my head again, like that will make it real. "I don't know . . . but he's a friend to me," I say, putting a splayed hand on my chest.

"Okay," Carlie says doubtfully. "But what about the asshat Brock?"

"I don't know why he's become fixated on me, but maybe now that he's been beaten twice he'll just . . . forget about me."

They look at me.

"Or not," Amber says in her droll way.

*True.*

We have a lull in our conversation and the sudden blare of the television constantly tuned to the news interrupts with a boom about the presidential-election candidates.

My bowel hiccups as my stepfather's face fills the screen.

My girlfriends are unaware of my inner turmoil and Amber turns away from the interruption with a bored grunt.

Then my face flashes on the screen: deep auburn hair, eyes so green they don't look real.

I make an instant decision, heaving my backpack off the table and pretending it fell. It crashes with a huge thunk and both girls turn at the distraction.

"Shit!" I say, like I'm pissed that tampons, lip gloss, my cell and wadded gum wrappers are everywhere to be picked up.

I'm not angry, I'm relieved as my stepfather fields questions about the election. And really low and quietly he answers, "Yes, the investigation to find my missing daughter is still under way and they have strong leads. Very strong leads."

His face fills the TV screen again and I feel his eyes on me, and through them, Thad's.

I shudder. Seeing my stepfather reminds me of the son. Why does Thad loom so large from so far away? Why can't I shake the feeling my hiatus from Thad is coming to an end?

A commercial break takes him away and I let out the breath I've been holding.

My friends and I collect the bag that spilled. I happen to look up and find Devin Castile's eyes on me.

With suspicion.

Did he see?

If he did, which part? The part where I purposefully dumped my bag, or the part where I felt I *had to* based on what was on the TV?

Pretty soon it won't matter; I'll be seeing him tonight.

Have you ever had an experience where you feel like you're moving in slow motion, as if traveling through water as you walk, or mud that you can see through? Well, that's what's happening with me.

I see Devin like a small black speck at the far reaches of the parking lot, gradually growing large as I draw nearer. Even from a distance I can tell it's him by the body language alone. He's casually perched against his big Harley, his arms folded across an impossibly broad chest, feet crossed at the ankles. He almost appears to be slumbering like a bear put away for hibernation. I know that's a façade; Devin is a lethal man. He's proven it already.

So why am I going with him to his apartment to finish what we began? To answer the sexual mystery my body yearns to solve?

The short answer is: *I want to.* That want has become a single drumbeat, drowning out reason, priorities and all common sense.

I keep swimming upstream toward him. The night is cool; autumn is in full swing, December around the corner as it snaps at my heels with an almost unpleasant bite.

We don't speak, our eyes never leaving each other.

When I reach him and he holds out his big paw, I come into the circle of his arms and he takes my wrist in his mighty grip and holds me still while he presses a kiss not to my lips, but to the base of my throat exactly on the hollow.

My pulse pushes against his lips as he lays soft pecks like fiery rain on the spot until my head falls back and he catches it with his free hand.

"We're going or we'll give people a show," Devin says against skin grown warm through his attentions. Then he lifts his head, his gaze pinning me intently. He grips my hair, just shy of causing pain, and says, "Promise me you'll never do that again."

*No more purse-bashing,* I translate.

I nod my head, his hand still buried in the tight plaits of my hair. "I won't have you in harm's way." He kisses the tip of my nose, then growls, "I can't protect you if you're walking in front of the truck, Jess."

*I didn't know he felt he had to,* I think as my body warms further from his admission.

I nod wordlessly. Devin moves to the Harley and swings a leather-clad leg over, straddling the long seat. With a hand he beckons me. When I'm close he scoops me behind him. I wrap my arms around his firm middle, the helmet a snug brain trap on my head as I press my face against his back.

As we roar off I catch sight of a lone figure standing in the middle of the large grassy swath that separates the dorms from the parking area.

It fills me with unease. It is the person's stillness that is noteworthy . . . and some kind of familiar something I can't put my finger on.

Maybe it's Brock?

*No,* I decide momentarily.

Then who?

I dismiss it as my increased paranoia has gotten to the red stage, alerting me so much that I'm almost becoming desensitized to the signals it sends me.

I don't know it yet, but I've put myself in the worst position possible. In worrying too much, I've overloaded my sensory input and become careless.

Just when I need to be the most vigilant, I've become complacent. I should have taken the breaking news report for what it was: an omen that after a two-year reprieve, the horror and misery are now coming full circle.

My mind leaves the person I saw and goes to more important matters.

I trip over the threshold of Devin's apartment and he jerks me against him to keep me from falling, which serves to press me against him, our bodies melded, hip to head. He floats me across a glossy wood floor, my toes not even touching the surface as his forehead remains bent and pressed against mine, his minty breath warm against my face.

He kicks the door to a large bedroom open and flings me on the bed, the gentleness of the preceding moment gone.

My heart rate jacks up a notch, my chest heaves and I scoot back instinctively. Castile frowns as he strips his leather jacket off, pulling off his tight black T-shirt soon after, taking it by the collar as all men do and tearing it over his nonexistent hair. His pants are next, kicked into a pile with the rest.

"No second thoughts, Jess," he says, a statement that vibrates with contained heat, prowling on his hands and knees across the orgy-sized bed, cornering me. I guess if you're as big as Devin is, you need all that room. I find my back crammed against the headboard and he smiles, the muscles of his pecs like hard balls of flesh as he pounces on me, hauling me against the bare skin of his torso and partway beneath him. I wrap my hands loosely around him, half hugging, half holding him off.

"It's been a while," I say softly, and he leans back, his eyes almost black in the low light of his bedroom.

"How long is a while?" His eyes study my face, searching for . . . I don't know what—guile? I don't have the heart of a manipulator even though I live a life in disguise; in my heart I'm honest. An oxymoron to beat all.

I'm embarrassed to admit my lack of experience and don't know if a throwaway of my virginity for curiosity's sake and a boyfriend who couldn't last through the worst of the Thad siege count.

However, Castile is waiting and I tell him the truth. "Two years," I say with hesitation, feeling inexperienced and suddenly foolish.

"How many lovers?" he asks as he seizes both my breasts and pushes them together through my light sweater, and I gasp at the suddenness of the movement. His fingers graze my nipples with a light touch, the flesh pebbles, rising to move into his nimble tweak and roll.

"Ah . . . ," I moan, and he smiles and growls, "How. Many?"

"It doesn't matter . . . I'm not asking you for a list of your lovers," I say, slightly indignant as he works my breasts over, his body covering mine.

"It's not a tally, I just want . . . I want to know how far we can go. If you're a novice, then I don't want to scare you off."

My eyes shift to his and whatever he sees there causes him to lift his head from the place where my breast swells to my nipple and laugh. It's hearty, full and real.

I can't help but smile.

"You're a vanilla girl, aren't you, Jess?" he asks softly.

I have a vague understanding that *vanilla* means "normal." So I answer, "I guess so."

"We'll change that, but not today," he says, his voice lowering as his lust heightens. "Today, I want to be inside you . . .

here," he says, pressing the width of his palm across the mound of my sex. It heats right through the denim; a small inarticulate sound of desire breaks the seal of my lips and he nods, all seriousness again.

"I'm going to take off your clothes now." Devin waits for my assent and I give it with my eyes. A part of me still can't believe I'm doing it and the thought shatters when he slowly unbuttons my sweater. With each button undone he moves to the next, lighting a kiss upon my flaming skin in a rhythm of one button undone, one kiss landing on my flesh like intermittent heated butterfly wings. When Devin reaches my belly button he licks a circle around the divot and I shiver. My hips involuntarily lurch upward, eliciting a low chuckle from Devin.

"My eager ballerina," he murmurs against my skin, throwing my sweater onto the pile of his own shed clothing. I sigh, taking my hand and moving it to his skull, which has a soft ebony shadow of growth on the top. Celtic tattoo symbols swirl at the base of his skull, framing his neck as it meets his head. I can tell he likes it as he puts the side of his face against my flat stomach, his eyes rolling up to meet mine. His hands hold the small mounds of my ass, gently kneading the flesh there, and I melt into the rough caress. We gaze at each other for a moment and he says, "I'm going to enjoy fucking you, Jess."

I move to sit up and he puts a staying hand on my belly, then adds, "Over and over."

I hate his words because they're delivered like a crass promise, but the effect is undeniable. My parts moisten, readying for what he says he'll do. The sad truth is no matter how crude the delivery, I can't stand the thought of his *not* fucking me.

I want to be fucked: *over and over*.

By Devin Castile.

He sees inside me better than I see inside myself and moves closer to my face. I think he'll kiss me but he surprises me again, lowering his head to a lace-covered breast and sucking my nipple through the material, and that imaginary thread is plucked like a guitar string; it runs back and forth with delicious heat from his suckling mouth to the bud of nerves in the soft cleft between my legs. I'm throbbing for him and he knows it. Never breaking his kiss of my breast, he undoes my pants with an expert flick and drop of the button and zipper, shimmying the jeans from my hips.

When my pants are at my ankles, and my matching lavender panties and bra are the only scraps of material between us, he glances at me from his position at my tit.

"Spread your legs, Jess," he says.

I resist and he sucks harder. I *so* don't like to be told what to do.

I don't move my knees apart and I can feel him smile against my breast like it's a game.

It is. The next moment his thumb is pushing my clit back and forth, through the material like he's doing with my bra, the nub so engorged with my arousal it is a terrible kind of pain/pleasure, and I groan, my hands convulsively clenching the back of his skull, pressing his mouth harder against my nipple. Instead of increasing the pressure on my nipple he completely takes me off guard. Lifting his lips off my right nipple, he moves to the left and does a featherweight tongue swirl as he whips his thumb across my clit.

Back and forth, back and forth, the material of my panties drenched with my own juices, the fabric sliding underneath the unrelenting pressure of his thumb in a delicious velvet friction.

I feel the orgasm of all orgasms beating along the edge of my consciousness and I grunt in frustration.

"Spread. Your. Legs, Jess . . . ," he commands with his own urgency, his breath coming in short pants.

I'm ashamed but I do. And not a little bit, but until I feel my feet at the edges of his huge bed.

"Thank you," he breathes against my breast, and in a smooth movement he leaves my clit and pushes the tiny strip of my G-string aside and puts his finger deeply inside me.

I come hard, my back arching. "Ah!" I scream in a hoarse yell that is both soft and shaky, intense and alive. My channel clenches the finger he has shoved inside me, my wet pulsating orgasm causing us both to groan against each other.

"Now . . . I fuck you," Devin says. He rises on his knees above me like a Titan, the tattoo sleeve on his dominant arm a mix of geometric symbols melded together, transitioning to band-type wrist cuffs. Devin leans over me, swiping a small wrapped foil package off the surface of his nightstand. He tears the wrapper off the condom with his teeth, blowing it out of the way, and sheaths it on himself with a practiced roll.

Castile moves over my body, my panties disappear and all I can do is look at him mutely, my channel still giving soft pulses of pleasure.

When he moves into the low bedside light I see his sprung dick. I gasp and no, *just no,* I can't take what he has. My eyes widen.

He reads my expression. "You can and you will, Jess."

I begin to move and he falls on me, the tip of his cock nudging my entrance. "I'll be slow."

I close my eyes as his cock takes the first sensuous inch of my entrance by quiet storm.

"Ah . . . ," I groan, my fear groundless as he's true to his word, the progress gradually widening me, filling me with his girth.

"Jesus, Jess . . . I'm not gonna last inside you . . . so tight, you're so tight," he whispers against me, his hips rocking deeper inside me and my sex stretching slowly to accommodate him.

I spread my legs wider, understanding his prep work: he wanted to make it good for me. He knew I'd not had sex in a while and wanted to give me pleasure.

Then he's at the end of me, his cock throbbing inside my deep wetness, the tip of his dick kissing my womb. He cradles my face, looking into my eyes.

The look is uncomfortably intimate and he pulls out halfway and thrusts into me like that, holding my face still with both his palms as his thrusts become deeper and faster and I become gradually unfocused as another orgasm builds off the first.

"That's right, Jess . . . just one more time," Devin says, and thrusts so deeply inside me it feels like his balls are inside me too, and he comes . . . and I yell out loud again, his shattering release bringing mine in perfect sync.

He swivels his hips inside me and I groan, my hips flexing against him as if they always have, a second orgasm exploding after the first. My mouth goes dry and I am limp, boneless and floating. A residual tingling like a low-level electric current has shorted me and I get a stupid grin on my face.

"Thank you, Jess."

I say nothing. It's impossible after what he's done to me, what he's torn from me that I didn't even know I had. *How can I ever be with anyone else besides him?* I think, my smile fading as he presses into my neck, his body softening inside mine.

Castile's it for me.

*I don't want a relationship.*

Devin moves to slide out of me and my body fights him as he does, clenching against his penis, and he laughs, looking down into my face. "It's like you're custom-made for me," he says in wonder, his smile lighting up every corner of his face.

I smile back at him wistfully, touching his face, the stubble rough against my palm.

If I don't want a relationship, then why do I feel so much like crying?

# TEN

I don't want to leave and know I must. It doesn't matter that it's Friday. I don't have ballet practice on the weekend but that doesn't mean I don't have barre time.

I'm already mourning the thought of leaving Castile.

That makes me realize something.

I turn to him, still naked. "I'm wondering . . ."

He smiles, all his attention riveted on our laced hands, seemingly fascinated by it.

I lift my brows.

"You're so tiny," he says with a laugh, his eyes crinkling at the corners, and I'm suddenly struck by the fact that he doesn't look like a college senior, but maybe older. I shake the momentary image away and then he just looks like Castile again.

I look at our clasped hands, my fingers swallowed by his. Then I think of how overweight I am for a ballerina and that old familiar shame instantly flows over me.

Devin catches my expression. "What is that look for?" he asks, letting our hands fall, a small frown landing between his eyes.

I glance away but can feel the pressure of the silence, commanding me to answer. It's not the first time I've considered why I always feel that I must answer when I'm around Castile. The answer is: I don't know why.

I never talk about my family. It's painful and I feel a weight descend on my chest. But somehow, Devin makes me feel better . . . feel *more*.

"Tell me, Jess," he says in a low voice of encouragement.

I give a small shrug. The sheet falls away from my breast and Castile bends to suck it into his mouth, effectively blanking my thought process.

"Tell me," he commands around my breast, and despite the fantastic tingling he's causing, I do.

"My family used to tell me I was 'too big'—*too fat*—for ballet," I say in the softest confessional voice I've ever used.

I feel my nipple pop out of Devin's mouth with a small release of suction. My eyes are clenched shut; it's all tactile.

"You've got to be fucking kidding me," he says.

I shake my head miserably. "No." I open my eyes and those deep chocolate eyes see into me . . . all the way in. I feel like Devin Castile can hear my heart beating as he sees straight to my toenails.

He cradles my head again and does something no one has ever done: he unbraids my hair, his fingers breaking each plait. "You'll wear your hair down when you're with me, Jess

Mackey." When my hair is a waterfall between us, he spears it with his fingers, gripping so tightly it's just shy of my pain threshold.

"Listen to me," he says, his eyes searching mine with an unnerving intensity. I gulp.

"Okay," I murmur. I couldn't go anywhere if I wanted to. I don't.

"You. Are. Perfect," he says with quiet emphasis. It stands between us with the resonating harmony of truth. I feel it thrumming through my body.

"Let me show you just how much." Devin moves to my toes and sucks the middle toe, and I gasp. He rolls his eyes to mine and I look down the line of my own body, between the peaks of my breasts, over the sheared mound of my pubic bone to his large hands, which cup my ass again. He's so tall he can grab my ass cheeks and suck my toes simultaneously. My breathing becomes irregular with his attentions.

It's sensual, not sexual, and I wonder briefly at the difference. Then his words shatter me along with his actions.

Devin Castile moves up my body with languid slowness, the ease of his feelings for me, our mutual chemistry, paving the way.

"You're perfect here." He puts a gentle hand underneath the bend in my knee and places a moist, hot kiss on the tip; moving on, he slides his palm up my thigh, stopping just short of where things get interesting.

"And here," Castile whispers, flicking his tongue against my inner thigh, and I moan my pleasure, my arms flinging behind my head as I try to stay still when my entire body wants to move against that gentle seeking touch.

"And here," he says in a tone I can barely hear. But hearing means nothing when I feel his warm tongue at my entrance and with a single pushing lap, he drives it up the middle of me and I shudder under his wet caress.

I forget that I'm not perfect.

In his arms, I am.

I follow Devin to his bike and pat down my carelessly braided hair. Without a hairbrush, I could only manage a single plait. I'm back to grinning like a fool, as sore as I can stand.

The wonderful kind. My aches are from my body's satisfaction.

I can still feel the rasp of his stubble against my lips . . . and not the ones on my face.

He turns and laughs at my goofy expression. He grabs me and pulls me against him, slamming his lips against mine, and I can taste him and myself.

It's erotic and wonderful.

"Did I make it good for you?" Castile asks, and I nod, shy again. He notices my braid and gives a small, almost disciplinary look of disapproval, and a flutter in my chest rises with the thought of my disobedience. My little rebellions thrill me and tease him.

I ignore his subtle reprimand and instead answer, "Very." I look up from beneath my lashes and his face blooms with a rare full grin, my vague insurgence forgotten.

Then a thoughtful look comes over his face. "What were you asking me before?"

*What?* I think in my postcoital stupor I forgot.

I suddenly remember what I was going to ask him before things got too hot for me to care. "Oh . . . it seems irrelevant now, but I think of you about half the time as 'Castile' in my head . . ." I waffle my hand back and forth. I just don't always think of him as Devin.

He chuckles and I give him a sharp look. "Actually, funny you mention it; I go by Cas to my friends."

"Really?" I feel my brows rise in surprise.

He nods.

"Cas." I try it out. I think I like it.

He pulls me closer and whispers along my temple, "Why don't you try using it when I'm buried inside you, Jess . . ."

I flush at the reminder of what we've done and when I look up I stare at those lips . . . I think of where they've been and the heat on my face deepens.

He chucks a finger under my chin and cups my ass with his hand. "Mine," he says, squeezing once hard, and slaps it quickly.

It makes heat spark where he just had his mouth thirty minutes before, and he sees the expression on my face.

His face grows thoughtful for the second time, darkening with desire. "Maybe not so vanilla after all."

I walk to the back of the bike without looking at him.

Because Devin . . . I mean *Cas* . . . he knows what I'm thinking somehow.

Always.

Cas walks me to the dorm entrance, opening the door, and I punch in my security code. When I turn he meets my mouth like we're in perfect synchronicity. My arms wind around his neck and I stand on tiptoe to reach him.

Reach him I do.

We pull away, breathless, my hand covering lips swollen with his kisses, the last one placing another tender layer on top of the preceding pecks.

"I'll text, Jess," he says simply, his body in the shadows of the dimly lit vestibule.

Then he leaves.

Cas leaves me in the foyer of my dorm. My body grows cold without the heat of his.

I turn away so he won't see the shine of my eyes if he looks.

I have a feeling he doesn't.

I open the main door and climb the stairs.

I never see that Devin Castile is indeed watching me. He stays in that spot for minutes after I'm out of sight.

I wish he stayed with me; I'm in for the fright of my life.

Moving down the long corridor of the dorm, I make my way to my room. The door is standing ajar and I sigh. *Damn thing, it never latches properly.*

I push it open and Mitch Maverick is lying casually on my bed.

"Hey, dancing girl," he says, and I quietly shut the door behind me.

I can still smell Cas all over my body, in my body—everywhere. I'm instantly on guard.

Why is Mitch in my room?

He sits up and spreads his hands away from his body. "The door was open . . . I couldn't get you by text," he says, making a lame excuse.

I put my hands on my hips. "I was out with Cas, I had it turned off . . ."

"Cas? You mean Castile?" he asks, and I nod.

"Yeah, it's his nickname," I say.

Mitch frowns, his pale eyes like a cat's in the gloom of my room. Disconcerted, I reach to turn on my bedside lamp. His casual invasion of my space is not cool. He studies me as I pointedly avoid his eyes. It's so awkward I can hardly breathe. I want to be by myself and think about what just happened to me. What I've done.

"Come on, Jess, don't be pissed. I had to see you!" he says, gathering me against him.

Of course, it's a shock after I've been with Cas, whose touch and body feel like I was meant to be against him, touched by him.

"Stop," I tell Mitch, and he backs away.

"What's the problem, Jess?" he asks, and those eyes seem to hold mine against my will.

"We were going to go out tomorrow night, right?" I remind him, my eyes trying to adjust to light from only the bedside lamp, watching his expression.

"Yeah, I just wanted to see you quick before tomorrow," he says, his eyes pleading with mine.

*Mitch is the safe nice guy,* I remind myself. I need to go easy.

I can't let the sexual consumption of me by Devin Castile put me off balance.

"Right . . . okay, just—text me or something. It was scary to find someone here in my room," I say emphatically.

His eyes shift away from mine to the doorknob. "You should get that fixed, Jess."

I lift my hands up in an *I give up* gesture. "I've got a work order in but they're not that concerned."

He laughs. "Typical school response." Then his expression grows serious. "But with Amanda's body found . . ."

I snap the main room light on. The glare washes over Mitch and a trick of the light casts a shadow over his usual pale gaze. I straighten and he does too.

I suddenly become aware of how tall Mitch is.

How he's in my room with me by myself.

"What is it?" he asks.

I shake my head; it's my paranoia again. I need to calm down. I clasp my hands together to stop their quaking. Mitch moves forward and rubs his hands up and down my arms. "It's okay. I know it's upsetting . . . but I'm here."

I look up into his face and he smiles, my sudden anxiety dialing down. I nod. "You're right. I can't believe they haven't caught this creep yet."

"Me either," Mitch says in agreement, raking a hand through his hair. "I haven't been excluded from the running already . . . ?" he asks, winking while he stuffs his hands in his front jean pockets, and I watch the muscles ripple. He's leaner than Cas but has the same sort of athletic grace.

I think about the last four hours spent with Cas, his body moving against mine.

Then I think about the promise I made to myself, the one he made to me: *just fucking.*

*It didn't feel like just fucking,* I think.

I stiffen my spine and squish my emotional roller coaster, banishing thoughts of one man while I stand in front of another. "No, not yet, Mitch."

He grabs me in a bear hug and plants a kiss on the top of my hair, and I wildly think I might smell like guy, having been plastered against Cas for hours. If I do, he says nothing, pulling away with a small secret smile.

Mitch puts his hand on the knob. "I'll text a time tomorrow . . ."

"Okay," I say, shutting the door behind him. I begin to turn away, then a knock hits the wood and I jump.

I open it and it's Mitch again. "Sorry about scaring you, Jess."

I smile at him. He's forgiven. Can't fault a guy for being eager.

*Or can you?*

"And get this knob fixed . . . anybody could get in."

The threat of what's happened on campus sits between us and I find myself nodding again.

He's right; I'm vulnerable without that lock working perfectly. I know from hard experience that most predators need opportunity. I certainly didn't want to give that to anyone.

I lay my forehead against the door, hearing his footsteps retreating down the hall.

*What am I doing?*

My cell vibrates; wedged inside the front pocket of my jeans, it trembles with urgency.

Keeping my head where it is, I snatch it out and bring it around in front of me, scrolling down the virtual path of messages.

I'm terrible at erasing them.

What r u doing? It's from Carlie.

Nothing, just got back from Cas's, I send back.

Who?

Oh yeah.

He told me I can call him Cas, I reply.

Are we looking for wedding dresses yet?

I roll my eyes even though she can't see me. She sounds smug even through the text.

No, gawd, remember? Just sex.

Riiggght! XO girlfriend ;)

She is such a pain in my ass. But I'm smiling.

Let's go out, she says.

K.

I push the cell back in my pocket and sit down on the rickety stool in front of my vanity mirror. My one braid is a thick mess, with more hair escaping than held.

I comb the mess with my fingers, trying to detangle it, and finally, when it's all untangled, I run a wide-toothed comb through it. Finishing there, I remove all my clothes, the panties last. I grin at how well used they look and throw them into the hamper with a content smile.

I take my makeup off with a wipe and reapply a little, combing my hair neatly, then mess it up to get it back in that half-done bun I like to throw it in just as Carlie knocks on the door. She strolls in without waiting for a reply.

I frown at the knob again and she sees my face.

"What is it, ya grumpy bitch?" she says snarkily.

I laugh. "Oh, that stupid knob . . ." I throw up my hands and tell her the hassle it's become.

Carlie's amused expression sort of fades. "I don't know if it's okay that Mitch was in here . . . I mean, stalker much?" Carlie says, twirling a piece of dark hair in a tight circle, then letting it spring free.

I think about what she said as I roll my lips together, applying the last of a barely-there-colored lip gloss. It promises four hours of staying power. Yeah, right.

"I don't know," I say, "I think he just . . . wants to win my hand or something."

Carlie looks at me, narrowing her eyes with more than a little suspicion, dismissing La Hunk for the moment. "Huh."

She suddenly brightens. "Well, how was it on your 'date' with Devin? Oh, I mean, *Cas,*" she says, all ears.

But I'm just not ready. It's still too raw . . . powerful. I can't diminish coming together with him by casually laying out all the gory details. It doesn't feel right.

I get cagey and she can almost see the curtains drop on my response. She holds up her hand. "Too new?"

I grimace. "Yeah." Images of his hands and lips everywhere, outside of me . . . inside, rise like the tide in my mind.

Carlie leans forward, watching my face. "I'm dying here: just give me one morsel, then I swear . . . I'll leave ya alone about it for like, five days."

I can't help it; I bark out a laugh, smearing the gloss on my teeth as I do.

We smile at each other and I say softly, "I don't want to be with anyone else."

Carlie's face falls. "Oh no."

I lock gazes with her and sigh. "Oh yes."

"That's bad," she says, biting her lip, then her eyes find mine again. "What about Mitch?"

I let the moment stretch without answering and her eyes grow wide. Carlie opens her mouth to speak but I answer anyway.

It's the truth for once. "I don't know."

# ELEVEN

⁓

*M*itch picks me up at the curb and this time, we're not going to Skoochie's. It's an unspoken consensus that it would be beyond awkward if I showed up there with my date when Cas bounces there.

*I don't share,* rattles in my brain uncomfortably again.

I shove it away and take a covert sniff of my outfit; I decide I smell like I always do after a shift at Java Head: coffee laced with vanilla. I'm a walking, talking latte.

Mitch greets me with a quick peck and shoulder squeeze, dragging me around to the passenger side, where he opens the door with a flourish, swinging his dark bangs out of his eyes, the pale orbs revealed like a curtain has been opened, silver dollars shining down at me.

"What?" I laugh.

He grins. "I'm taking you somewhere nice . . ."

"Oh?" I look down at my short skirt, black opaque stockings

and heels, the straps twining around my ankles like slinking snakes.

Mitch's eyes travel my figure, and when that light gaze reaches my face again I blush at his pleased scrutiny.

"You look perfect."

I think of Cas instantly, telling me I'm perfect in a soft moment of confidence. I cast my eyes down, willing myself into the moment with another man. It's more of an effort than I care to admit.

Mitch puts a gentle finger under my chin and our gazes lock. "What?"

I shake my head gently and say, "Nothing."

He gives a sardonic tilt of his lips and says, "If you say so."

"I do," I say, slipping into the Camaro and shutting the heavy door behind me.

Mitch gets in the car and slides behind the wheel.

"Where are we going?"

He winks. "You'll see."

⁓

I let my held breath out at the view. It's Tideland's at Redondo Beach, a little pocket of Seattle. A finger of the city of Kent travels here but technically it's really in Des Moines. It's strange what a person finds out when they're going into hiding. I considered pretty much everything about the area. I looked at many different places to settle and finally decided on the University of Washington. I can't lie to myself; the decision was motivated by distance and underlined by beauty.

As Mitch guides me to our table, I take in walls that are made of not drywall but glass. They are the frame for the ocean, and beyond the vast grayness of the churning water, the Olympic Mountains rise like great snow-capped jewels of icy aquamarine, the sunset washing them with shades of tangerine, hot pink and gold. As I look, the imagery becomes a little disturbing. The whiteness of the snow is washed in the deepest red before night settles.

It looks like spilled blood.

I give an involuntary shiver and Mitch leans in next to me. "Cold?"

I give a tiny shake of my head. Swinging my hips, I gracefully sit in one motion and Mitch pushes in my chair.

He really is perfect for me: cultured, lacrosse athlete, scrumptious to look at, thoughtful . . .

But he isn't ready for my secret and he isn't Cas.

I know that Devin Castile is temporary. That it's a game of sex and chemistry. Nothing that hot can last; it'd be spontaneous combustion.

I look back into Mitch's eyes as he quietly orders wine that I'm not old enough to drink. Somehow, the waiter misses carding me.

Could it be the fifty-dollar-per-plate price tag? I guess when the restaurant is pulling in that kind of revenue, they can overlook pesky things like underage drinking.

"So how's ballet, Jess?"

I play with the stem of my wineglass, watching the deep burgundy slide and slop inside the fine crystal, my short natural nails pink against the translucent stem.

"It's good," I say.

"Really?" Mitch drawls, leaning back.

I laugh. "No . . . it kinda sucks, actually."

We look at each other. "Why?"

"Is lacrosse difficult?"

Mitch's eyes change from soft to hard instantly. "Yes."

I lift a shoulder, watching his eyes latch on to the skin exposed by the peekaboo design of the shimmering silver material, and answer, "Ballet is the same."

"I watched you dance at the tryout."

I wait for him to expound and Mitch doesn't disappoint.

"You were made to dance, Jess." He leans forward with an unexpected intensity. "In fact, I'm not sure why you're in college at all. I'm in lacrosse because I got a scholarship and it's paying my way, but what's a future in lacrosse?" He gives an easy laugh that sounds like a snort. "There's no career." His eyes land on mine with weight. "But you . . . you could be that. A dancer."

I nod; it's all I want. But already I'm older than I should be. I lost two years hiding from Thad that I can't get back. But now I have my chance, and I'm not going to lose it for anything.

That TV screen with dear old stepdad springs into my mind again and I ignore it.

"School's just a fallback." I look into his eyes and see his encouragement, so I go on. "I love ballet, but let's face it, I can't dance forever . . ."

"How long?" he asks.

"It depends on the dancer . . . maybe midthirties?" That seems so far off but I watch people age all around me. I won't be immune. I might be twenty now but too soon, life will take me for a spin and I'll be old.

Mitch takes my hands across the tablecloth, the moon a witness that illuminates the water in a faintly glowing pumpkin color. "Let me share your life, Jess."

I look into Mitch's eyes and immediately want to draw away, my panic at divulging details an all-too-familiar defense mechanism. Anyone gets too close, and I instantly pull back.

He intuits my retreat right away, gripping my fingers tighter, and I make a small distress sound. He releases me just as the food comes and I gratefully concentrate on my plate.

"Jess," Mitch says softly as the waiter moves away into the shadows to await our slightest demand.

I force my eyes to meet his.

He smiles and I give a small smile back. "Too fast?"

"Yeah." I laugh a little. "I'm not ready for . . ." I wave my hand back and forth. "All this," I say, looking around at the rich food, the shining silver cutlery, the cut glass and flowers on every table.

"Should I just go for it then?"

*Like Cas,* is the unspoken end to that question, and I get angry, my hunger and promises forgotten.

I let out a huff, putting my fork on the plate in the proper position, right side up, tines left of center, handle to the right. His eyes flick to my small, unconscious movement, then lift to meet my eyes.

"I like you, Mitch, I do. And I'm going to be honest."

"That'd be nice," he says with thinly veiled sarcasm.

I lean forward. "This was your idea."

He sighs. "True, go on."

"I have an arrangement with Cas." I let the statement stand there between us like a glass wall. As impenetrable as any but frustrating because you can see what you want so clearly.

He wants me.

I want what Mitch offers.

I want what I'm doing with Cas like I want my next breath. Right now, at this very moment, I feel like he's my food and drink.

It's beyond confusing,. But after two years of avoiding intimacy like the black plague, I've suddenly found my selfish streak. If these two men can live with my terms, then maybe I'll let it play out.

"Say the words, Jess," he tells me.

I fight to look into his eyes. "We're friends."

I let the look say what else we are.

"You're screwing him."

I flinch; he notices and doesn't back down.

I flush, fighting the urge to fidget with my hands. Instead I shift in the restaurant seat.

I don't owe him. *I do.* "Yes," I say.

"Damn it." He seethes.

"So don't date me," I say softly, praying that this won't be our last date, praying that he'll wait through my unhealthy infatuation with Cas.

"You can't just be with him," he says.

"I'm . . . I can't . . ." I stutter, flustered.

"Be lovers with two men?" he says for me, and I nod.

Mitch laughs. "Oh, I don't know, you're doing a bang-up job right now."

I cast my eyes down at my salmon, a small portion the size of a deck of cards, slathered with butter and sprinkled with lemon. Exquisitely prepared. Red potatoes and fresh asparagus flank the salmon in a perfectly orchestrated arrangement of color and symmetry.

I'm no longer hungry but Mitch leans forward, stabbing a piece of my fish and shoving it into his mouth, where he chews it viciously, his eyes glittering as the candlelight shadows his gaze as it pierces me.

"Well?" he asks, dabbing his mouth with his cloth napkin. His eyes hold a dare.

I flip my fork upside down, then right side up on my plate. Back and forth, back and forth. Mitch sets his tines on top of my own, stopping the nervous motion. His brows rise in question, but he says nothing.

I can't do this. *Can I?*

"I don't know . . . Cas said"—and this part sticks in my throat; I feel like I choke but spit it out anyway—"he won't share."

Mitch grins. "Bullshit."

My eyes jerk to his.

"You're telling me he's not banging every female that *he* wants?"

I feel instant betrayal pour over me and I'm suddenly off balance, almost swaying.

I haven't thought about it. Maybe he's sleeping with everyone. I feel the heat rush over my body and settle on the fair skin of my face again. I've been had.

Of course a guy like Devin Castile can have anyone he wants. Why would he settle for a secretive ballet dancer?

Mitch lets me think about it and sees when I decide.

"Good," he says. "I was hoping you'd see things my way."

"What about you?" I ask, my eyes searching his.

He shrugs. "I don't need anyone else, Jess. Pretty soon, you'll get that." He gives a disgusted sigh. "When Castile gets tired of you and throws you away, I'll be here to catch you before you fall."

"That's a crappy thing to predict," I say with heat.

"Let's just say he's got a rep and I doubt he's going to suddenly give up his swinging-dick agenda for you."

Mitch has a point. It's bordering on unkind but I can't dispute the logic right now. He's right. I don't know Cas.

My body does.

And my body is in love. Will the heart follow?

We eat in an uneasy peace. Did I just agree to date two men? One who all but told me he wants to be with me and *with me*?

Further, am I really going to be with them both?

I watch Mitch eat with gusto. Now that he's gotten that off his chest, he is relishing the expensive supper. I shift mine around on the plate, Mitch's big bite missing from the fish staring back at me. The fish dares me to finish it.

I can't.

Should've turned tail and run while I could.

⁓

"Again!" Boel barks, and we spin, dropping like clumsy cattle, our chests heaving, so out of breath we're gasping.

"Ugh!" he says, gliding away angrily. If anyone can glide away angrily, it is my instructor. He's had it with us. It's *so* Monday, my strange weekend put away like a jacket in a closet, to be pulled out later and inspected for unseen lint.

I was strangely languid this weekend and didn't do any barre exercises.

"Miss Mackey," Boel says, snapping his fingers at me like I haven't been paying attention.

Right.

"Yes, Instructor Boel," I say, rising en pointe, then landing, rising, then landing, trying to stay warm for the next move of torture that will be asked of me.

Then he is suddenly there and I yelp. His hand grabs my thigh and I groan. I am sore and exhausted and he knows right. Where. To. Touch me.

"Are you working your four hours?" he asks, tightening his hold, and I bite my lip.

Shelby gives me a look of sympathy, then her eyes widen.

A hand falls over Boel's; the ebony tattoo band rises above Boel's wrist.

"Let her go or I break it," Cas says casually. But his eyes aren't casual, they're lethal. Serious.

I breathe a little easier when Boel lifts his hand and turns to face him. Cas steps away and squares off with my instructor. Though he's muscular like all dancers, it's a lithe build, muscles strung taut and fashioned by many years of movement, not building. When compared with Cas, who is six foot four or thereabouts, he looks like a pony next to a thoroughbred.

Boel's eyes narrow on Cas; beginning at his feet, they ride up to his head. Finding he likes nothing about Cas, he dismisses him. "I am in the middle of a ballet class that is not to be interrupted by anyone, understood?"

Cas walks into his chest, looking down on Boel, who, to his credit, doesn't give an inch.

"Whoa . . . who's this guy?" Shelby asks.

Who is Cas? My lover . . . my . . . I don't know. A guy I just began sleeping with? I don't know how to quantify it and we aren't in junior high anymore. He isn't a guy I "like."

"I just began dating him . . . ," I answer quietly.

Shelby gives me a look. "He's gonna fuck up your chances."

I've thought of that, my thigh still throbbing from Boel's abuse.

"What I understand is that you will not put your hands on Jess again. Do *you* understand?"

Cas waits and Boel deliberates. Surely he sees that Cas might be a problem.

I knew he would.

"Who might you be?" Boel finally asks.

I groan out loud and they both ignore me.

Cas's eyes flick to mine.

Oh no.

"I'm who she's seeing, Instructor Boel."

Boel stares a heartbeat longer; both of us are surprised he knows Boel's name.

"You have me at a disadvantage . . . ," Boel says.

"Devin Castile," Cas says.

Boel smiles in a condescending way. "I'm sorry, I didn't recognize you as the young man that Miss Mackey is seeing."

*Oh shit.* Shelby gives me wide eyes and I stare back, our
ballet gear growing cold against our body during the alterca-
tion. My temperature drops and my body gives a small shake,
becoming chilled.

"The one I know she is dating." Boel gives me a murder-
ous glance that clearly says, *You could have been doing barre this
weekend instead of him.*

Although that unspoken sentiment is presumptuous, it's the
truth. My shoulders drop and Shelby gives me a conciliatory
pat.

Cas's brows lower over his eyes, his tattooed arm clenching, the muscles bulging in response to the tension of the
moment.

"I believe his name is Maverick. Mitch . . . yes?"

I want to die. Cas looks over at me, then back at Boel.

Then he says the unexpected: "No matter who your dancer
is screwing, you won't lay hands on her."

*Oh dear baby Jesus.* My heart stutters in response to his
words.

"You cannot tell me how to teach ballet. You are obviously
no expert."

Cas scoffs, folding his arms over his tight T-shirt. "I know
a thing or two about pain, Boel." His eyes meet Boel's. "Giving
and receiving."

Shelby gives me a considering look at that bit of strangeness.

"And her face told me you were hurting her. Dance with her, fine, but if you touch her again . . . I might see fit to make dancing harder for your arrogant ass."

I put my face in my hands. I've *so* opened Pandora's box. And found Devin Castile inside.

# TWELVE

~

"Jesus, Mary and Joseph," Shelby says, making the sign of the cross. "That guy is smokin' hot!" she yells in the cavernous communal bathroom as she mock-fans herself above her crotch and I wince at the echo. The two of us strip down to naked, my bath tote in my hand as I swing it over to my stall and jerk the spigot hard to the left. It protests with a lurching groan as hot water pours out.

"He . . . like, handed Boel his ass!" Shelby pumps her fist down low, then spears the air with it in a victor's pose.

I roll my eyes. "Right, and now Boel hates me and is going to cut me from the program." I stand under the spray, shivering the instant the water hits my chilled skin. Then slowly my flesh heats and I lather the soap, getting it everywhere.

I turn and Shelby's staring at me, mouth open.

"He's not gonna give you the ax. You're the teacher's pet."

I smile, washing the shampoo out of my hair as Shelby steps underneath the spray.

"We're not in elementary school," I say.

Shelby laughs. "True dat . . . but I know where I stand, Mackey."

I startle at my old nickname—now surname—coming from her mouth. Blinking the hot water out of my eyes, I look at her through the rising steam, our naked bodies as starved and sore as they can be.

"What are you talking about?" I ask cautiously.

She squeezes out a quarter-sized amount of green shampoo into her palm and carefully lathers it, working it into her hair incrementally.

I wait, then she says, "I know I can't be principal." Her eyes meet mine. The silence that was so restful, just two dancers getting clean, is now strained. "You have that thing, Jess. That"— she makes her hand move one direction, then the other—"indefinable spark." Shelby shrugs. "I don't. And that's okay. I'm just sayin'"—she looks at me with serious eyes—"don't blow it because of a dude. Even if he is a walking sexsicle." Shelby giggles into her soapy hand and I know it's going to be okay.

But I don't know for whom.

Not me. I've pissed everyone off.

Boel is mad because my boyfriend, who is actually *not*, threatened him. Mitch is mad because he wants to *be* my boyfriend but I'm the lover of another. Shelby noticed my placement of importance with Boel without words.

And Cas can follow me by scent alone. Like a bloodhound, he's hot on my trail.

My ballet potential lies in the hands of Boel, who is moody at best; I'm barely staying on top of my classes and horribly distracted by Cas.

I probably ruined everything by running out of the gym while they argued, Shelby coming after me.

We rinse off.

Shelby uses her towel to pat her body dry, then flips her head upside down and wraps her hair in it. It's such a long-haired-girl move that I laugh.

"What?"

I grin. "Conserving towels?"

"Hell yeah. I don't want one more thing to have to wash. It's a damn hassle. Plus, the laundry room is frigging creepy as hell." She shudders. Then she levels a look at me. "We can't hide in the bathroom forever."

I sigh, patting my hair dry and slicking it into a bun. I don't want all the wet hair helping to freeze my ass off in the December chill factor.

"It's like my mom says: 'Better face the music.'"

Right.

We get dressed and walk out into the hall. And Boel doesn't disappoint: he's out in the hall, tapping his foot, eyes like steel, and all for me.

"Catch ya later, Jess," Shelby says as she scuttles away, chancing a furtive glance at me before disappearing.

*Coward*, I think. Not that I can blame her.

My eyes shift back to my ballet instructor and he meets my gaze across the corridor. "You either agree with my methods or quit, Jess," he states.

I open my mouth to defend Cas and realize there's no defense.

"I won't go easy on you." His eyes drill mine. "I will check for muscle soreness, which should be lessening if you're working the barre as I've directed."

I stare at my feet.

"That's what I thought," Boel says, a subtle reprimand in his tone. Then he says, "Sometimes dancers need a tonic."

I look up with a question in my face at his bizarre comment.

His lips twitch at my expression. "It isn't necessarily good for them. Tastes good going down, leaves them vaguely poisoned but they still want more." His serious eyes lock with mine. He continues slowly. "The more they have the more they want."

*Cas, he's talking about Cas . . . like a metaphor.*

I blink and he nods.

"I don't want him interfering with my teaching again, Miss Mackey." And I can tell he's thinking about saying more. When he finally does it's not what I expect.

"Think moderation on that beverage."

Boel walks away, his smooth grace showcased as his form grows narrower when he moves farther down the corridor.

I thought he'd say to shut Cas out. That he's bad for me.

It's not that Cas is good for me, not really.

It's that he's good for the dancer in me. Ultimately, that's all that Boel gives a shit about.

I walk down the corridor after Boel, noticing that Cas is nowhere to be seen. He appeared like a ghost and disappeared like one.

He's an enigma.

I look at the big D circled on my midterm paper and want to burst into tears. There's no overcoming that. I obviously suck and am going to draw attention to myself because I am challenged by biology.

I can't believe it. There are mouth-breathing jocks in here who are acing—*acing*—damn biology. My eyes stray to Brock's group unconsciously, then I look back at my paper. I know I'm smart; why can't I do well?

*I know why.* I'm just not through lying to myself.

"Nice grade, dancing girl," Brad murmurs. His own paper shows a red-penned B+. I want to judo-chop him in the throat. It's worse when he grins at me. I scowl at his grinning face.

"You know, Brad . . . I want to kick your ass but I know you can take me," I say sulkily, crossing my arms in front of my chest.

He guffaws, a real shout-out, and the professor takes a break from his lecture to give Brad a look.

Brad slinks down in his seat and covers his mouth, his shoulders shaking at my expense, his laughter barely contained.

I listen to the lecture as my B+ neighbor takes half-assed notes.

Yeah.

Finally biology is over and Professor Steuben stops me before I can escape. Brad makes a fake gun with his hand and pulls the trigger, snickering as he skulks out of class. *He's always shooting me,* I think as I glare at his broad departing back.

"Miss Mackey," Steuben says.

I swing my eyes back to his. "Yes?" I ask, but I know.

"Let's meet in my office for a quick chat, shall we?"

That's one of those questions people ask you that doesn't require a response and is decidedly beyond a suggestion. I feel my shoulders fall and he gives me an awkward pat. "It's not as bad as all that. However"—his kind gaze studies my face—"before it becomes something insurmountable, let's squelch it."

As I follow Steuben, I feel eyes burning a hole into me. I turn, and there's no one. My class has exited and the next class is filtering in. As Steuben passes his TA, he says casually, "Give me ten minutes and begin on the review."

I get depressed immediately, shaking off the disconcerting feeling of being watched with difficulty.

He opens the door and we walk in together. Steuben gestures to the seat in front of him. "Have a seat."

I sit.

"What's the trouble, Jess?"

*I am hiding from my powerful and psychotic family, I'm dating two guys, having sex with one and debating having it with another while dancing for a premier ballet troupe under the unrelenting instruction of Patrick Boel. I couldn't make a clear choice for my own benefit if a gun barrel was pressed against my head.*

*Oh . . . nothing.* Aloud I say, "I'm busy and having a hard time with the Punnett square." *Less is more,* I tell myself.

His brows furrow and he leans forward. "Do you need a tutor?"

*Hell no.* "I think if I give it a little more attention I can make this up."

Professor Steuben gives a minuscule shake of his head. "I'm

not sure. You'll possibly pass, but I've taken the time to look over your transcripts, and you have an exemplary record—"

"I'll try harder," I say, interrupting, as I force every ounce of sincerity that I can into my expression, keeping my scattered thoughts at bay by the slimmest margin.

He watches me again, gauging my truthfulness. "Then come to me when you have a question. The offer for tutorial assistance still stands, Miss Mackey. Here at the U Dub, we take education very seriously." His gaze weighs me down and I drown, trying not to gasp for air.

"Thank you," I choke out. I know he means well. I just can't . . . have another complication added to my life or I'll scream.

I should have just stayed in my shell where I was safe.

It was stupid.

I won't know how much until after.

Carlie files her glitter nail tips and I find myself stuffing a pang of envy; with dance there is no way that I can have the fancy nails. They look beautiful though.

She blows on the tips and sparkly purple dust falls softly to the creaky wooden floors of her shared dorm room. Amber will be back any minute, so I crank out the story of my dressing-down by not only Boel but Steuben as well.

"Hell, girlfriend, aren't you in a titty clamp today!" Carlie cackles as she carefully inspects the tapering at the sides of the square tips. When I don't respond immediately, her eyes raise over the talons of her nails and meet mine. I don't even have the heart to laugh and I fight squirming.

"So . . . what's the deal with La Hunk?"

"The deal is he still wants me."

"And you're boinking Cas?" Carlie laughs, rubbing her hands gleefully together as she tears through her nightstand drawer. When she finds what she's looking for she lifts it in the air triumphantly.

Condoms. "Look"—she waves the box around, its dual colors blurring—"a color for each guy! Damn, girl!" She continues, utterly immune to my gaping mouth. "When you decide to ditch celibacy, you do it in style!"

Her grin slips when she sees my face.

"God, Jess . . . I'm sorry!" She runs over and hugs me. "I want two studs to breed me, baby! Tell Carlie all about it."

So I do.

I endanger Carlie's life with the truth and we're never the same again.

We sit silently until a text buzzes and Carlie looks down, expertly tapping out her response with her long nails; they've worn the keys' colors off by now. She refuses to get a smartphone; she fears her nails will wreck the screen.

Beauty is pain.

"That was Amber," Carlie says, her eyes searching mine. "We have time."

We look at each other.

Finally Carlie says, "I feel like my bullshit meter just got busted."

"Nope."

"You're the presidential candidate's daughter?" Her eyes bug, then she adds, "The one who has been missing for the last two years?"

I nod.

She studies me. "I guess I can see it . . . but here you were, under my nose, and I never knew. I mean . . ." She looks at me again and I flinch at the accusation there. "You could've told me. I mean, hell!" She slaps her hand on the nightstand, the small cosmetic items rattling on the surface. "I'm your friend, Jess." I watch as a lipstick teeters on the edge, then falls on the floor, making a loud clunk.

"Faith was my friend too," I say, and the first tear climbs out of my eye and runs down my face. It trembles on my chin and wets my hand when it falls. "She was my friend too," I whisper.

"Oh, baby . . . come here," Carlie says, and hauls me against her.

I cry for a long time; Carlie holds me, and I let her because I'm selfish.

And for the first time in two years I really begin to live. The secret has been killing me. Taking small chunks out of who I am until I wasn't me anymore.

I was nothing.

Carlie pulls away. "Jewell MacLeod."

I nod, swiping the hot trail of sadness away with my hand.

"Jess . . . Mackey." Carlie cocks her head.

"It's my nickname."

"Mackey . . ." Carlie tries it, then nods her head, her curly hair bouncing on her shoulders. "*Jess* just didn't work."

I roll my eyes and she laughs. "You didn't know!" I say, and she smiles.

"Mackey works, and I can call you that and no one will be the wiser, right?"

I deliberate. "Yeah, it should be okay."

Then she asks me the worst thing: "Who was Faith?"

When my lip trembles she throws her hands up in reassurance. "You don't have to . . ."

I gulp back the lump in my throat. "No. I want to." We stare at each other. "Faith deserves it."

I tell her and watch as she absorbs the murder of my friend, my hands twisting into knots, loosening, then twisting again.

When the last word drops from my mouth like a time-delay bomb, I realize that Carlie will go to the authorities and tell them that I let my best friend die, that I hastened her death through my inaction. That it's time for the MacLeods to reclaim me like a lost prize.

But she does none of that.

Carlie is more like Faith than I realized. She clasps my hands to her chest and I feel her heart beat against our twined fingers.

"She knew, Jess . . . she *knew* when she came the risk it could be. You warned her and she came anyway," Carlie says, her expression full of emotions I can't assimilate, can't own.

"I knew she would," I say in a hoarse shout that makes Carlie wince, my grief a raw and untrained thing. My throat convulses from the sheer effort of punishing myself by withholding tears that need release.

"Knowing and doing are two different things, girlfriend,"

she says softly, cupping the side of my face with her hand. She continues, her voice a fierce thing whipping me. "You need to stop hiding. Go to the police, tell them what happened, what you heard."

"They let Thad go."

Carlie looks at me.

"I didn't see anything . . . I just heard, I heard . . ." I can't finish; the panic attack has come and set up camp. I tear my hands out of Carlie's and fall to the floor, the breaths wheezing in and out of my tortured chest, my airway a tight tube without a hole.

"Jesus, Jess! What the fuck is it?" Carlie's hands flutter around me like helpless birds in a cage.

I count, my palms smacking the wooden floor, then I close my eyes, concentrating on my breathing. I count backward while Carlie tries to give me mouth-to-mouth and I bat her away.

"Panic . . ." I gasp and she lifts her mouth off mine.

"What?" she screams.

"Attack . . . ," I say.

"Oh . . . you scared the piss out of me. That was a fun little slice," Carlie says. She sits back on her haunches, hands quaking while her dark eyes regard me, wide and tense in her expressive face.

I lie there for a second, then finally . . . slowly sit up, taking a deep lungful of air as soon as I'm upright.

"Why?"

"I don't know . . . when I think about . . ."

"Faith's death." Carlie says the words I can't.

I nod. "That night . . . I can't breathe."

"Well, the more we talk about it, the less that's gonna happen, right?"

I think about it. I don't know. I've never told before.

Carlie gives me a fierce hug, then sets me away from her. "Tell me the rest."

I take several calming, deep inhales; Carlie does it with me like we're at a labor class for expectant mothers.

Then I tell the rest.

I don't have another attack, though I do take several breaks to move through my fear.

My grief.

My secrets.

# THIRTEEN

*O*ur tears soak our mingled hair, dark chestnut spiral curls against my fake dark blond. When the last of my sadness has echoed in her tight quarters, Carlie leans away and we sit there in diminished silence, both feeling wrung out.

"Well that's a ball buster," Carlie says.

I raise my hand and she gives a wan smile. "Yes, Mackey?" Her brows rise, trying for coy and not quite making it after the heaviness of my revelations.

"I don't have testicles," I say in a deadpan voice.

We bark out laughter and Amber walks in.

"What'd I miss?" she asks, slamming the door with a hip and flopping on the floor, crossing her legs.

"Nothing," I say too quickly, and Carlie gives me a sharp look.

I wonder if she'll tell.

She doesn't.

"I was just saying I didn't have a nut sack . . ." I let the words trail off.

"Huh," Amber says, pursing her lips. "I thought you'd stay classy, Jess . . . but you've been hanging around us for too long and you're sliding down the slippery slope of Potty Mouth."

"Potty mouth?" I ask.

Amber begins to expound and Carlie puts up her palm, stopping her midcomment. "You don't wanna know."

"Stay classy, that's all I'm saying!" Amber says.

"Girls!" I yell, and they look at me. "Let's talk about more important matters."

"'Let's talk about more important matters,'" Amber says, parroting me. "What are ya, my mother?"

"No . . . but we don't have to talk about balls if we don't want to."

"I want to," Amber says, and we laugh.

And it's all right for now.

It's been days since I've seen Cas—since he "came to my rescue," then disappeared.

It makes me vaguely uneasy. Where does he go for these minivacations? Of course, that falls under "intimacy."

A thing we've agreed not to exchange.

One minute he's protecting me and the next he's a ghost.

I give up, telling myself it's perfect that he doesn't fill my cell with his texts. His declarations of concern, love . . . romance.

Questions I don't want to answer. Can't answer.

I grump through the halls, swinging my tote out of the way as I travel through the horde of other zombielike students. It's almost Friday and we all feel ready for the weekend.

A bright spot clouds my vision.

I'd know that dark, longish hair anywhere. The broad back faces me, jeans tight in all the right places, worn from use rather than money, and I glide quietly up behind Mitch.

I hear him say something that gives me pause, my steps faltering.

"No, she's not remotely suspicious . . ." He nods into the cell.

*Is he talking about me? Or is that my arrogance speaking?*

Then he huffs out a sigh, raking a hand through his hair.

A habit I found endearing that now makes me think it's more about nerves.

When anxiety is at its height, people tend to manifest it physically.

Like my fun little panic attacks when my mind tries to circle that last memory of Faith . . . and Thad.

He nods tersely, then answers in the affirmative since the caller can't see him. Another hand rakes through his hair. "Soon . . . I told you, it's not time yet. Chill, bro."

Mitch lowers his voice. "I know you want it perfect. Me too. How come you think I waited this long . . ."

There's a pause as he listens to the caller.

"Yeah," Mitch answers. "Stop calling . . . text instead."

He looks at his cell, giving an exasperated shake of his head with a disgusted snort.

Mitch punches a button on his smartphone and the screen

falls to inky deadness. He shoves it into his pocket and I instantly try to arrange my features into neutrality. Never an easy thing.

Mitch's eyes widen when he sees me. A shadow of some emotion I can't name flashes through them and then is gone.

"Hey, Jess," he says, his smile lighting up his pale eyes with warmth. I can almost see his internal monologue: *Did she hear that conversation?* Or maybe I'm imagining too much.

"Hey," I say hesitantly. He comes toward me, wrapping me against him. "I was just going to text you."

"Yeah?" I ask, a little breathless, knowing I heard something I shouldn't have. I can't banish the thought that it might have been about me.

Maybe it wasn't. I can't ask; I'd look like a loser with a capital L. One of those nosy chicks that no guy wants to be with.

"I got something important to do, you want to come with me?"

I say, "Sure," before thinking about what it might be.

We slip out of the campus hand in hand, my bitterness over an aloof Devin Castile slipping away with Mitch's warm hand in mine.

We get to his car and I drop inside, kicking off my shoes and throwing my feet up on the dash. I curl my sore toes by reflex, always happy to be out of the confines of footwear.

Mitch slides in and gives a small frown, and I lower my legs. "Got to treat the girl with respect," he says as a joke, but I know he means it. I watch as he gives the dash a stroke with a lover's hand.

I stay quiet over his weirdness about the car. I guess some guys are touchy with that.

His strong hand goes to the ignition and turns the key; the powerful low drone of the engine thrums through the interior of the car. Heat pours from the old venting system. It bathes my feet in liquid warmth and I sigh, curling my toes in spontaneous pleasure for the second time in minutes.

"They hurt?" Mitch asks when he sees my expression.

I nod, then think of something. While he's backing out I say, "I need to be back by three thirty for dance practice."

"Ballet," he says, seemingly correcting me, and I give him a puzzled look. The way he says it reminds me of something, a wisplike memory that slyly evades me; the harder I chase it, the thinner it becomes, until I can't find it, though it feels important.

I huff and sit back against the seat, kinda miffed at myself and my muddled brain.

Kinda pent up. I can't help but think of Cas and what he could do to ease me and I smile a secret smile. In another man's car. As if Mitch knows I'm thinking of Castile, he tears out of the parking lot in a spray of gravel and dirt; my hand automatically latches onto the side handle on the interior of the door. Mitch grips the wheel, spinning it with expert ease, and I watch those long, tapered fingers work with finesse, wearing his car instead of driving it.

"What's going on, Mitch?" I ask. What I really want to ask stays stuck in my throat.

What "she" was he talking about? Why is he pissed and driving like a maniac?

"You'll see," he says cryptically, and I do.

In a matter of minutes a cemetery rises up in front of us like the ground vomited it out.

I think of the last grave I visited. It's like a trigger, and I swallow my memories and emotions like the bitter pill they are.

He can't know. Mitch has another reason for bringing me here.

I'm dying to find out.

We pull onto a long black ribbon of asphalt. It twists and twines without end, and finally we pull up to a small knoll. He shuts off the car and we get out.

Round sprays of flowers garishly display themselves as we slowly weave our way to a fresh grave.

He pauses in front of it, jamming his hands in his pockets.

My eyes travel to the headstone, which reads:

TAWNY SIMON

1990–2012

BELOVED SISTER

BELOVED DAUGHTER

INTERRUPTED DESTINY

It is so painful, so acute, that I have to turn away. I grit my teeth against it and turn to watch Mitch, his brows drawn low across those light eyes, the line of them a perfect picture frame. He looks like a dark angel standing there, the gray Seattle skies perfectly showcasing his coloring while his gaze broods into nowhere and his hands flex inside the denim as if trapped.

"Who is she?" I ask.

He turns that blazing gaze on me and I take a step back. "My sister."

Mitch turns away and I think about how much it would take to bring me out here to her fresh graveside. The pain that he's kept buried.

He is trusting me with his sorrow.

I turn to him and put my arms around his waist. After a moment's hesitation, he puts his around me.

"She was my half sister," he says against my hair.

I lean back, still safe in his embrace, searching his face so I'll say the right thing. The words that would soothe and affirm rather than harm.

But he speaks first. "She was whole to me." His fists clench against my back and he gives me a hate-filled stare.

Not for me, *at me*. It's different.

"She was one of the first last year . . ."

*The murders.*

That's why he was so over the top about getting into my room, why he's so overprotective.

He takes his arms from around me and grasps my hands.

Looking into my eyes, Mitch watches me assimilate the intimate confidence. He puts our knotted hands against his chest. "Now you see why I am the way I am?"

I do.

It makes me feel even more torn. I have no right to question this man who has just survived the tragedy of his sister getting killed so viciously.

He gives a small, self-conscious lift of his shoulders and says, "I wanted you to know."

I let my head fall forward against his chest and he presses my face against the warmth of him. "I'm glad. Thank you for trusting me."

We kiss over his sister's grave, his tongue pushing past the barrier of my lips. He's expert, insistent and perfect with his method. A small tingle starts up where my heat lies in wait for the right match to strike.

*It's not enough.*

This man who wants me, he's extended his trust but can't flip that invisible switch.

I mourn that. Cas isn't right for me but he's the only one who can scratch that unique itch.

But he sure isn't sharing his life with me.

It deepens my indecision instead of clarifying my choices.

And soon it *will* be a choice. It doesn't matter that Mitch will share me and Castile won't. One will have to go to make room for the other.

The kiss breaks like a brittle stick and we walk hand in hand to the car.

Mitch walks around to the driver's side and slides in. I glance behind me once, expecting to commit to memory the sight of Mitch's lost sibling's grave.

Instead, I see Cas standing like a black statue, piercing all the gray around him, an ominous ebony stripe against the pewter sky. I leave the door standing open and run to him.

"Jess!" I hear Mitch yell, and I turn to him.

"I'll be right back!" I scream.

That prick! How dare he ignore me for days after what we

did, then reappear when I'm out with his competition? And excuse me! Zero class! He shows up at the graveside of Mitch's sister . . .

My opinion of Cas drops further and, of course, my opinion of myself.

When I turn back to give him a piece of my mind, he's gone.

I move to where he was and see depressions of footprints but nothing else.

Mitch rushes up next to me. "What is it?" he asks frantically, thinking the sky is falling or we're in mortal danger.

"I thought I saw someone . . . ," I say as my voice trails off.

"Who?" Mitch asks with deserved irritation running through his voice.

"Nobody," I say, and walk away.

I guess there are such things as ghosts.

But this ghost is going to give me answers, golden dick or not.

⁓

"Let me come in for a little while, Jess," Mitch says against my temple as he squeezes my hip bones through my jeans.

"No," I murmur as his hand moves to cup my breast through the fabric of my knitted sweater, and I gasp. Our breath is fogging up the car windows and I keep myself in check. I might not have the electric chemistry with Mitch that I have with Cas, but there's something there.

"Why?" he asks, caressing my nipple through the fabric. It rises, begging to be touched, and he obliges, pinching it almost savagely; my eyes pop open. "That hurts," I say.

"Sorry, it's hard not to be enthusiastic with you, Jess. You're so sexy," Mitch breathes against my shirt, which he's pulled up to my bra, his face against my belly.

I'm suddenly uncomfortable with the quick turn the make-out session has made. I begin to pull down my shirt and he stops me.

"You know you want to . . . I thought we already talked about it, Jess." He continues the pecking assault of the flesh between my ooh-la-la and the thin strap of material that holds my breasts.

We did . . . I mean, I agreed to . . . what *did* I agree to?

He unsnaps my jeans and it's like cold water thrown in my face. *I have dance practice,* I think randomly.

I also have an epiphany: I am major crushing on Devin Castile even if he's ignoring me. It is *so* in the way of everything else. Including this.

I hold Mitch's wrist as he tries to cram it down the front of my jeans.

"Come on, baby . . . I let you in," he pleads.

I meet his eyes. "I'm sorry about your sister, Mitch . . . I am."

*She's not remotely suspicious* . . . Mitch's words from the over-heard cell conversation slide through my mind.

"But I am not going to do a mercy fuck in your Camaro."

*The car is more important than me . . .*

Mitch recoils like I've slapped him. I instantly regret my thoughtless words.

*I don't want to have sex in the back of a car in the university parking lot.*

Mitch sighs, his hands leaving my suddenly cold body. I can see his erection like a rigid pole underneath the denim of his jeans and avoid breathing a sigh of relief by sheer willpower.

I jerk my sweater down and button my jeans, my face heating.

I didn't feel cheap while Cas made love to me. It was amazing, intense . . . and in the end, the most intimate thing I'd ever done.

*Why do I feel cheap with Mitch? He's offering me so much more.*

"You need to go to dance," Mitch says in a flat voice.

My face crumples. "I'm sorry . . . I don't want to do it . . . here, and it's . . ."

"'Too soon'?" he guesses, making air quotes.

"Yeah," I say in a small voice.

"Fine." His face closes down and the eyes I thought were like a warm pool of comfort are now like ice chipping at my soul.

I turn and smoothly jerk the handle on his car door, stepping out. Then I hesitate.

*What the hell.*

I slam the door of the Camaro and walk briskly away.

Fuck him.

And fuck Cas too. *Although I already did that, didn't I?*

I dance my ass off at practice and receive the first genuine smile from Boel I've ever received.

I'm angry and passionate in my rage. Shelby steers clear of

me and Boel keeps smiling as I lash my pirouettes, attacking my dance steps with precision and focus. When he grabs me to dance, I meet him head-on like a battle opponent.

When Patrick Boel lifts me I am unafraid. His eyes widen at my ferocity but he engages me and we dance.

I finish and stomp out without a word to anyone.

Maybe I don't need men. I can just dance and concentrate on school.

That's what I'll do.

I know an empty promise when I hear one.

I know I can't keep it when I see Castile standing across the hall as I exit the showers.

We stare at each other for moments that seem like hours.

I don't know who moves first but before I can take my next breath I'm in his arms, his fingers tearing out my damp braid and plowing through my long hair. He holds my face, slamming his mouth against mine until I groan and open it for him. His other hand goes to the small of my back, then dives down to my ass as he lifts me against him, my legs automatically winding around his waist.

"Where?" he asks breathlessly. I utter some unintelligible sound in the back of my throat as he presses me against the wall, fiddling with a knob, and then I'm inside a dark, confined space; the sharp smell of pine and cotton fills my nostrils.

"No!" I half shout.

"Yes!" Cas says, his forearm an ass rest as his tongue moves over my collarbone.

"Are you fucking him, Jess?" he asks, his forehead against mine, his forearm pinning me against the wall; as my heart beats against him he wedges his knee between where my thighs split and that delicious weight settles in there from the hard contact.

"Are you?" he removes his hand and grinds me against the cinder-block wall and I cry out, my channel giving a single pulse of need and heat as it drives down my body.

His deep brown eyes, outlined in the gloom from the light that seeps underneath the door, pierce me like a sword through my body. I can't breathe or think for the need.

"No." I grind back, my body a soft and supple weapon against Cas and his hardness.

"God, Jess . . . you're killin' me," he says, giving me a reactive hip thrust back, and we both gasp at the electric connection, my hips cradling his erection, lock to key.

"Say yes," he pleads.

But not like Mitch.

"Yes." I breathe my assent and he strips me in seconds. Plunging his hands under my ass again, he surprises me by kneeling before me in semi-worship.

"What are . . . ?" I say, and his mouth is on me.

"Oh . . ." I moan, my head falling to the side against the cool textured concrete of the wall, my hands finding their way to the stubble on top of his head.

"Put your feet on my shoulders," he growls, and I do. He nibbles at my lower lips and little tethered shock waves run through me in trembling pulses; my legs begin to shake and I know he's bringing me.

Just as I'm on the brink of coming he stands, laying me on a surface . . . I don't know what . . . and I don't care. The juices of my arousal coat his face and he licks them with his tongue as he pops his dick from his pants.

"I'm going to fuck you now, Jess," he says, his face a mask of hard planes and unyielding, tightly contained emotion.

"Okay," I say in languid resignation as my hand floats up; I wrap slender fingers around his shaft and he throws his head back.

"No . . . you don't," he says, and he's in me, the thick blunt end of him begging at my entrance, and I spread my legs wider. He grabs my ankles and rocks deeper, his eyes never leaving mine.

"Watch me, Jess," he says in quiet command, and I don't look away, can't. He pulls out torturously slow, then slams his cock so deeply inside me my walls clench around him and he moans softly, the beautiful ebony of his eyes disappearing when he closes them in paused ecstasy.

When he opens them, his cock retreats from against my womb like a warm tide, to rush deeply inside me again. With each thrust he rocks us closer to that mutuality that you only hear about.

And that's what Cas and I have: synchronicity.

He grabs my face, his hips burying him inside me again and again. I feel his cock harden even more and know he'll come.

He stiffens above me, his eyes fluttering, the sooty lashes feathering closed on a face that's at once relaxed and tense. He brings me over the edge, like the ocean sweeping over a bluff.

The crashing waves of my orgasm engulf me, lifting me to the surface of a detached and beautiful satisfaction. A completeness.

Instead of drowning, I float.

I don't react when Castile brings me against himself, holding me with a tenderness reserved for lovers.

Not casual sex partners.

If he held me any tighter we'd be one person. I say nothing and listen to our hearts beat together in perfect harmony.

I just let Devin Castile take me to the moon in the custodian's closet.

The irony isn't lost on me.

I smile and snuggle closer as Cas presses a warm kiss to my temple, then another on the healing wound of my cheek before he tucks me in against him.

*I still don't feel cheap, I feel cherished.*

# FOURTEEN

⌇

I realize I'm basically naked, that my clothes are hanging off my body instead of *on* my body. The loop of one of my bra straps dangles off my shoulder. I sit up in Cas's arms and he gives a low chuckle, giving me a short, hard squeeze before letting me up.

I look around at the inside of the closet, feeling horribly vulnerable.

I just screwed Cas's socks off . . . after I promised myself that I'd get my questions answered.

*Clearly, that isn't happening.*

And on the heels of that little revelation:

*Gawd, we didn't use a condom.*

I hear the snap of a lighter and a flame illuminates Castile's face, the square jaw hardly moving as he takes a drag of his smoke.

"You're not smoking in here," I hiss at his flagrant disregard for rules. Rules of any kind. It's easier to focus on that.

He gives me a puzzled look, then stares at the cig. "Doesn't look that way."

"Somebody's going to smell that, Cas!"

He takes another drag and the tip glows red, his inhalation making it fiery orange for a moment, then he snuffs it out.

The darkness descends and I dress quickly.

"Wait," Cas says in a low voice when I move toward the door to escape what we've done, what I know I'm too weak not to continue. Tobacco, male, soap, sweat and spice are a unique mixture of scents now burned into my memory . . . the smell of Cas.

He tackles me from behind, my palms slamming into the door, and I want to weep; I want Cas so bad I can hardly stand it. I try to protect myself even as I wish for more of the same kind of harm only he can give.

But I know he doesn't want me. It's like that invisible glass wall stands between us. A hammer won't shatter it . . . but maybe my heart will break.

Cas puts his arms around me, cupping my breasts and burying his lips against my neck.

A little pathetic sound escapes me and he tightens his hold, blowing hot breath against the sensitive flesh of my throat. A riot of goose bumps breaks out.

"Don't see Maverick, Jess."

I stiffen in a muscular embrace that feels like flesh encased steel. All that strength has been against me, moving with a tenderness that belies the contained violence I know is an inherent part of Devin Castile.

"No," I say, knowing Cas doesn't realize that Mitch is putting on the full-court press to consummate a relationship that is moving too quickly. I've yet to make a choice.

But one might be choosing me whether I like it or not.

Cas nips my neck and the gooseflesh travels, spreading and growing. I can't help it; my head falls back to give him better access.

"You came in me," I say in accusation while he eats, pecks and licks at the neck he just attended to moments before when his flesh was a part of mine.

"Yeah," he says, and with great deliberateness I pull away, his hands caressing me as I turn to face him.

"Ah . . . pregnancy?" I state.

He looks down at me with unnerving intensity.

"STDs," I say, begging for a reaction.

His eyes glitter coolly in the dark and I seethe. "Can you say something, Cas?"

"I don't want anyone but you. Only you," he says, and caresses my face, his hand moving down to cup my chin, a rough thumb moving back and forth over lips swollen from kisses.

"You're lying," I say softly, those eyes on mine.

"I'm many things, but I'm no liar."

He bends to kiss me and I let him, his lips moving over mine, savoring them slowly.

When his head rises I back away. "We can't do this!" I say, my hand covering my mouth, the heat of his lips burning against my skin.

He cocks a brow, putting a large hand next to my head as he backs me up against the door. "Which part?" he asks. Then he puts his hand on me, cupping the sensitive mound of flesh between my legs, and I gasp at the contact, my sex pleasantly sore from his attentions earlier. "This part?" he whispers, kissing my forehead with a featherweight's press of his lips. "Or this part?" He leans in and kisses first one eyelid, then the other.

I can feel his lashes like silk lace against my skin, heating where they stroke, then they move until a path of fire has been laid where they've been.

"Or this?" He straightens, swinging his palm at the humble surroundings.

I sigh and fidget, flustered. Castile undoes every single strand of logic I possess, unraveling them without mercy.

"Which part did you not want to do, Jess?"

I can't answer, I can't look at him.

"Don't you want to fuck me, Jess?" he asks softly as he bends down, lifting my chin with a finger, his eyes pegging me to the spot. It isn't dark enough to hide his expression. "Don't lie, I deserve more," he says.

"Yes," I whisper reluctantly.

"Then tell me what. The. Problem is," he demands, his voice threaded with anger.

I instantly turn the tables now that our passion has cooled. My frustration with him hasn't.

"Why were you following me?"

He gives a disgusted grunt, scrubbing his skull ruthlessly and stepping away. I see the lie before he tells it. "I don't know."

I stalk him, moving back into that intimate space. It's not sexual now but filled with a different kind of heat.

"Tell me," I say, leaving off the *I deserve more*.

"I can't say," he says in a low voice.

I stand there in disbelief. He wants this casual thing we have between us that is anything but casual, on his terms. He gets to fuck me when he wants, where he wants; tell me who I'll date, who I'll screw (him); and follow me around without reason or accountability.

"No," I say, my own voice matching his pitch perfectly, but filled with anger and something I don't want to recognize.

Regret.

"No . . . Jess, *wait!*" Cas says, his hand grabbing my shoulder, and I shrug it off, whirling on him, and look up . . . way up.

"No! Casual I agreed to; this domineering caveman thing without commitment? Ah . . . no." I put my hand on the knob and think that he'll grab me again.

Hold me prisoner with his heat and kisses on my body.

I'm pathetically disappointed when he doesn't. I twist the knob in self-disgust and step out of the closet and into the corridor.

I pause, seeing who's standing there, Brock's expression one I instantly recognize. It takes me all of two seconds to scream.

It's cut short by a hand. It backhands me and my head slams so hard into the wall that it rings. My vision doubles and I slap my palm out, hitting the reverse of the same wall that I'd been pinned against with Cas.

I feel my body half collide, half slump against the cinder blocks and wonder vaguely where Cas is.

There's a dull roar in my ears.

It's Cas.

I hear flesh beating on flesh and don't know any more. My

brain is closing down in protection mode, the spiral of my thoughts leading down a long funnel of black.

My last thought is of Castile; I lied to him and myself.

*I love him,* and that is all.

～

"Is she gonna be okay?"

I hear low voices murmuring around me. I feel like I'm underwater and hear people's muted conversation from a distance. I swim to the surface.

*Cas.*

Cas is here.

My eyes open and the blurry surroundings shift and my vision sharpens.

*Hospital.*

I raise my hand and an IV bag is holding court beside my bed.

*My contacts.*

*They could type my blood . . . DNA.* All sorts of conceivable ideas that would reveal my secrets pop into my polluted brain. Maybe I'm just paranoid. Why would they think to check anything? I try to calm myself with logic. I'm sorting it out when I catch footsteps making their way to the bed.

My heart speeds up and the monitor shrieks its despair into the sterile environment.

Hard and heavy, those steps draw nearer.

I turn my head and wince; it hurts.

Cas swims into my vision and he smiles at me, his face

wearing the evidence of fists. I take in his split eyebrow and tracks of stitches that bisect the ebony perfection at the top of the arch. His lip is twice its normal size; a cut that has a single stitch protrudes from the skin in a standing unwieldy spike. A jagged cut is a lightning strike against his skull. My eyes travel to his hands and I see most of the skin of his knuckles is gone, some on his left hand, all on the right. Even his pinkie finger has been relieved of its flesh.

Hands that were expert and tender when he touched me.

My lip trembles at the disaster of his face and with a shaky exhale, I burst into tears.

"No . . . shush . . . I'm here, babe, I'm here." I feel the bed depress as he sits on the edge of it, gathering me against him, and the monitor shrieks a second time when my heart rate goes too high.

Cas jerks the monitor's plug out of the wall and it falls silent. A nurse enters and takes one look at the all black and leather that is Cas, his face a beaten mess, his six-feet-four, two-hundred-thirty-pound body bent over me, and says, "You, out."

Cas stares at her. "I will if Jess tells me."

They look at me.

"I don't think Miss Mackey is in any shape to decide anything of the kind."

I look into Devin's face. His battered face. "Did you . . . ?" I swallow and try again, my throat parched. He hands me a cup, pushing the bendy straw against my lips. The water is heaven as it slides down my throat. I nod and he takes it away, never removing his arm from around me. "Did you save me?"

He stares at me. Finally, he gives a nod.

I close my eyes.

"Let him stay," I say.

The nurse gives a snort of indignation, striding to the monitor and plugging the electrodes back into place. She turns on her heel with a huff and closes the door. It's almost a slam.

Cas's lips curl into a smile. "Battle-ax," he comments, and I laugh again, making my head throb. I grimace and his face turns serious.

"I'm sorry," he says, and I press my finger to his lips.

"He only got the one hit in, right?" he asks anxiously.

I nod. It was a good one. I don't remember anything after that.

A thought occurs to me. "How many?"

Cas looks uncomfortable, immediately understanding what I'm asking. Finally, he answers, "Five."

Five against one. Bad odds.

I swallow again, fearful. "Where are they now?" I ask because I must. It's shades of Thad and I'm scared all over again.

The ghost of a smile brushes his lips and is gone before I think I've seen it.

"Here," he says, one terse word.

"What?" I ask, sitting up quickly and looking around for the group to spring out like a jack-in-the-box toy.

Then it dawns on me.

We're in a hospital.

Devin Castile hurt them. Badly.

A small part of me is glad and I'm ashamed.

"How?" I ask, shaking my head. How does one guy take on five? It doesn't seem possible.

Cas shrugs. Then he looks off, his gaze riveted to the window. "When I saw that dickhead Brock hit you . . ." He lifts a shoulder, the muscles flanking his neck a small rolling mountain. "I saw red. I literally steamrolled them. In fact"—he gives a nervous chuckle—"I don't really remember doing much of it."

He palms his chin with an agitated hand, then lays his abused fist against his knee, the elbow sticking out at his side like a wing.

An angel's wing.

"I'm sorry I . . ." I don't know what to say. I unfold my hands and let them fall limply by my sides, thinking about the words I hurled at him before he beat five men to defend me.

"It's okay, Jess."

*He is so what I don't need,* I think, *and everything I do.*

"I know you need more than me."

My eyes jerk to his, my very thoughts laid bare from his mouth.

He laughs. "You oughta think about stuff with a straight face. You're an open book."

*Oh.*

He touches my face, then lets his hand drop with a laugh. "It's okay, it's what I like best about you."

I smile, thinking he has a funny way of showing it. My face heats with my recollections. I trample my thoughts savagely. "So . . . where do we go from here?" I ask.

Carlie storms in just as Cas opens his mouth and she

nearly shoves him away. "I know you saved her ass but . . . shoo, *hero!*" she says, and he laughs and backs away, giving her center stage.

Tears shimmer in my eyes; it feels so much like a good-bye I almost leap out of the hospital bed.

Somehow, I restrain myself, even when he gives me a little salute with two fingers and walks away, the leather creaking as he moves down the hall.

I swing my gaze away from Cas's retreating form reluctantly.

"Mackey?" Carlie asks, her eyes searching mine, her fingers in a death grip on my shoulders. "Girlfriend . . . you are *so* lucky!" She hugs me and I cave against her.

"Guess what?" she squeals. I blink stupidly and shake my head, so overwhelmed by the events of the last few hours I can't think.

"They've arrested Brock."

*Well thank God.* I sit there stupidly, waiting for the other shoe to drop.

Her eyebrows pop and her chin kicks up. *Uh-oh.* "Right, I guess you hit your head harder on that wall than they thought." Carlie gives a supreme eye-roll and I want to hit her; she makes me crazy sometimes.

Instead I cross my arms. "Spill it."

"For the murders."

My mouth gapes. *Oh my God . . . Amanda and the other girls . . . it was Brock all along.* I roll it around in my brain for a moment, but it doesn't hang right. Like a window shutter that's crooked.

"What?" she asks, frowning. "It's like great news. Stud saved you and Brock the Jock is a serial killer."

It seems a little too neat. For one, I know how a killer thinks . . . intimately, and Thad was smart. Covered his tracks, deliberate, methodically planning everything out. I lived only because I was too difficult to get rid of.

Faith wasn't.

I gulp, my hands trembling. I knot them together. "I don't think it's Brock, Carlie."

Carlie steps back, jutting her hip out, one knee flung to the side as she taps her foot. "Girl, you need to think about this. Brock is gonna make big rocks into little ones. Chicks are safe . . ." Then she smiles. "And the douchebags are gonna get it too."

"The other jocks? Brock's friends?" I ask, confused. She leans forward and in a conspirator's tone says, "They didn't *know* Brock was going after you, the asshats."

"What did they think they were doing?" I ask, perplexed, thinking of Cas beating all five.

"They thought they were gonna jump Castile."

People are seldom brave as individuals, but in groups, they are invincible.

"So Brock convinces them that they need to beat up Cas . . . Then he hits a girl, and Castile freight-trains on their asses!" she squeals, clapping her hands together, and gives a celebratory hop.

Something's not adding up. Brock was a royal dick. True. Cas had made him look bad. Brad did too. He was on my radar to avoid at all costs.

I'm almost there on working it through when Carlie asks, "So I heard you guys were found by the janitor's closet."

I keep a straight face but my skin is the tell, flaming to a high red, and Carlie bursts out laughing.

"Slut!" she hisses in glee.

"Takes one to know one," I whisper back with a smile in my voice.

She grins. "You're okay, Mackey."

I smile.

I will be.

# FIFTEEN

⁓

The entire university campus is in high spirits. Brock is the scapegoat and has been pinned with the rape/murders of a half dozen girls since 2011 while his cadre of mouth-breathing friends got off relatively unscathed. Only guilty of not knowing what Brock was really up to. That and the holiday break coming has made for a student-body euphoria.

I still wasn't buying it. The evidence was circumstantial and it was entirely too easy for my taste.

Or my brand of inert paranoia. I don't know what part of me can't stomach Brock being the one. But I can't. Even his interest in me, threatening me . . . seemed false, forced somehow. Did he scare me? Well, yeah. But *why* did he focus on me? And I still can't shake the feeling that Thad is somehow here, though I know he's not. Then a sly voice inserts itself within the already complex paranoia that has set up house, *maybe he's found me?* Don't the deaths bear too much similarity . . . to Faith's murder? Am I putting too much weight in the coincidence of it all?

I ask Brad in class, for once talking after the lecture instead of during.

He looks over at me, boots stacked underneath the seat in front of him. "Jess . . . he was an all-around dick. He has a thing about females. Equal opportunity. He killed those girls. 'Kay? Who knows how many he's done something to without killing them? Bad stuff, ya dig?"

I do.

Brad is a good guy, and Brock isn't. It's obvious. But a date rapist is not a serial murderer. For one, I don't think Brock is all that bright. Thad is. I keep coming back to the only point of reference I have. It isn't speculative either; I have firsthand knowledge. Living with Thad, observing his perverted nature, manifested in his cruelty toward anything that was living and he deemed beneath him, which, as it turned out, is a broad category. No, Brock seemed like small peanuts against my point of reference of Thad. Very.

I did some cursory research and serial killers usually have a borderline-genius IQ.

I know from hard experience Thad does. When I was little and I found the dead bodies of animals Thad "experimented" on and he threatened me, I knew. I knew if I told I'd end up like them. So I told Faith about it to stay sane in a household where eyes like a storm watched me. Threatening pewter clouds roiling in my direction, ready to rain on my head at the slightest provocation. When the sexual intimidation began, I had nowhere to turn except to Faith. She was intimidated by no one, nothing. At the end of our relationship it had become less equal, between her and I. Faith's concern for my safety, and for my parents' willingness to not see what was right underneath their noses drove Faith to confront Thad—she felt I had no other advocate. Neither one of us could have ever foreseen what would happen. I don't think Faith ever thought she'd die that day. We all think we're immortal. But Faith's fragility was proven out.

"Hey," Brad says.

"Huh?" I lift my head and realize he's called my name a few times.

His eyes latch on to mine and don't let go. "What is it?"

I shrug and give a nervous smile. "I think they've got the wrong guy, is all." Brad opens his mouth and I interrupt him. "He's a bad guy, but he's not the killer."

"The cops have evidence, Jess," he says with the gravity of truth behind him.

*I bet they do,* I think, still an unbeliever.

Then Brad gives me a sideways hug. "I'm glad you're okay and that jackass is where he deserves to be." He winks and it's case closed to Brad.

I sit and stew.

Brock's not innocent, but he's not guilty of this. Then who is? My heart screams Thad; my mind says no. Maybe my intellect is trying to protect my frail emotional framework.

I leave biology, thinking about Cas, who's disappeared again. I'm more confused than before, if possible. I almost run straight into Mitch, who catches me by the shoulders.

I look up at him and give a slow blink; my thoughts have been elsewhere.

"Let's talk, Jess," he says.

My body coils with anxiety; I clutch my backpack reflexively.

I knew this was coming. I can't handle the two men. I couldn't handle what happened with Brock . . . with Cas. But for two different reasons.

I resign myself to being late to my next class; my grades are suffering for so many reasons. It'd be easy to blame it on dance. But the reality is the distraction of Devin Castile and what he brings to the table, or doesn't bring . . . has changed my focus. It's moved from survival and anonymity to wanting to be with him. On whatever pathetic terms he dictates.

I walk beside Mitch and wonder where we'd be if there was no Devin Castile. Would I be in a romantic relationship with Mitch Maverick? Cruising around in his vintage Camaro, visiting a dead sister's grave, then taking in the fancy restaurants he somehow manages to afford?

I don't know because there *is* Cas. It's like he's always been. Like my life started when I met him. He's the man who woke me from the sleep of my existence. For that one thing I'll always be grateful.

*Tawny Simon*, I think suddenly. His sister's killer has been found. I turn to Mitch as he opens the door ahead of me. "Brock's been arrested. Tawny's killer is . . . he's going to prison," I say.

I don't really believe it's Brock but everyone else does; he's been arrested so it's official, right?

"Yeah," Mitch says, then in a flat voice he says, "That son of a bitch."

Hmm . . . doesn't sound like he wants to talk about it. Then his eyes are on me like pale strobes. "I wanted to talk about the other day. And the day that Brock paid you and Castile a visit."

*Shit-damn-shit.* I so don't want to talk about Cas and me.

We move outside as the other students flow through the courtyard, oblivious to two students standing in an awkward pairing underneath a tree that's littered its leaves all around us. They crunch underfoot as I shift my nervous weight. I think it's bizarre on about a hundred levels that he doesn't want to air his relief that there's closure to Tawny's death.

But he blows me away with, "I know about the closet . . . you and Castile screwing in there."

I'm speechless, robbed of my reaction. I can feel my throat closing up and fight off a panic attack. I don't know why I'd get one when it has nothing to do with memory triggers of Thad or anything like it, but I fight it, breathing deeply.

I don't owe Mitch an explanation. He looks at me like I'm some slut and it makes me angry. Who's the pushy one? Not me.

I feel my eyes narrow. "'How are you doing, Jess . . . since you were *attacked*,'" I say, seething at him. "Or, how about: 'I'm so glad my sister's *murderer* has been caught.'" I huff and fold my arms across my chest, cradling my breasts. "Why do you care about me and Cas? And"—I stab my finger in the air, ignoring his expression as it darkens—"how about you trying to get in my pants no matter what I want, huh?"

He moves in against me and I am suddenly afraid. This guy I thought was hot, gentle even, is now all hard angles and angry planes, his light eyes a fierce blazing fire in a face whose mouth has turned up in a leering snarl. "I should have fucked you right then. Why not?" he says, flinging his hands out, and some students who are mindlessly trudging turn to stare. "You'll fuck anyone . . . anywhere, right, Jess?" he says with soft menace.

I back away and my mouth drops open.

*He doesn't know me.* I was attacked by a fellow student who's now been arrested for the murder of six female students and he's worried about my closet activities. How come I didn't see it?

I did see, but I ignored it. The car, the pricey venues . . . his pushiness with sex. Like it was expected. That if he condescended to date me, he got to screw me. As it turns out, he doesn't want to share either. It isn't somehow hot, like Cas made it sound. Mitch makes me feel like he's peed on me. It feels dirty.

I feel dirty.

"I'm not going to dignify that with an answer," I say as rage drips from my voice. I go to turn away, hurt and confused, shame a close friend. I know my behavior with Cas has been erratic and spontaneous. But I'm not Mitch's girlfriend, not quite yet, and he doesn't get to lay claim to me by putting me down in front of the student body and marking his territory with his dick.

He takes a long step and grabs my elbow, the strength of his grip like a band of metal around me.

"Let me go, Mitch," I say in a low voice, holding outright fear off by the skin of my teeth.

"Yeah!" I hear Carlie say. "Let her go, ya cock juggler!"

"*Jesus,*" I breathe like a prayer as he releases me.

Mitch turns on her, then he looks at all the students around us, and they're all staring at him. He glares at them. Eyes that were beautifully light now appear as slits of unrelenting silver.

"Whatever," he says, flinging his hand out. "We're done here."

I just stare at him as Carlie comes from behind me. "Jack wagon," she whispers.

Mitch gives a last dark look in my direction. Carlie flips him the bird and he stalks off.

She searches my face, then asks, "What the *fuck* was that about?" Carlie looks around, seeing some rubberneckers still lingering, and says, "Piss off, show's over."

They wander off as the time for class has come.

"You're going to be late for class, Carlie," I say.

"Fuck that," she says, and winks.

I burst into tears.

"Ah, come on, Mackey, you're tougher than that." Carlie takes me into her arms, holding me as I cry.

Two women comforting each other.

I pull away.

"Tell Carlie, baby."

I do.

She listens, fuming more with each word. "Well, damn!" She gives a stomp of her high-heeled boot. "That peckerwood."

I snicker and she cracks a smile.

Carlie shakes her head. "It doesn't make sense. Mitch is smokin' hot, right?"

*I thought so.* "His behavior's not. It leaves much to be desired."

Carlie's brows draw together. "That's a weird-ass expression."

"My mom used to say it a lot," I say before I think.

She gets a sad expression. "I'm sorry you had to give up your family, Jess."

*Me too.* "My mom made her choice . . . and it wasn't me."

Carlie's eyes meet mine. "You love her."

I nod. "Yes."

She sighs. I watch her breath puff like a plume of icy frost when she exhales. "I don't know what to say about Mitch, Jess."

"He's an assclown?" I interject.

Carlie laughs until she wipes her eyes. "He's definitely that. He seemed so into you though." She looks at me. "Now he's decided he's pissed about you and Castile after he said, 'May the best man win.'" She drops her hands from the air quotes she made. "I don't get it."

"Me either, but he won't be getting in the golden panties . . ."

Carlie looks at me. "I've definitely been a bad influence."

I nod and grin. "Definitely."

"Sluts unite!" she says.

I agree, high-fiving her. It's a lame attempt to make me feel better about getting dressed down in public but it kinda works.

I guess life has made the decision for me after all. Mitch thinks I'm not worth pursuing because I did Cas in a closet.

She loops an arm through mine, escorting me to my next class, gruesome physics. "So how was the closet?" she asks innocently.

"I'll never think the same way about cleaning again . . . ," I say with a sly glance.

Carlie barks out a laugh and the wound that Mitch laid on me begins to slowly heal. There are scars beneath but this latest hurt won't become one. Because I have her.

And a little bit, I have Cas.

~

I check my phone and there's no text from Cas. *Where is he?*

There's a text from Mitch. My finger hovers for a second, then I swipe it across the screen, erasing it. Erasing him.

*Like I want to say anything to him.*

I admit I'm a little curious but if he's going to take more chunks out of me? *No,* better never to read it.

I stuff my cell in my gear and hoof it to dance, my bun trying to come loose as I slowly jog to the auditorium.

Boel's in a vile mood, pushing Shelby and me until we think we'll die, or wish to.

At the end of practice when we limp toward the door Boel says, "Miss Mackey?"

Shelby says, "Better you than me."

"Yeah, *thanks,*" I say. *So not funny.*

He faces me, uncomfortable. What? That's my job. I dump my gear at my feet and he looks pointedly at my face.

At the healing mark from Brock.

"I've heard about the episode."

*Brock getting arrested.*

His eyes darken. "You seem to be a magnet for dangerous men, Miss Mackey."

I don't know what to say. I'd like to refute it. But there's Brock.

Then there's Cas. Did he hurt me? No. Is he violent?

Oh yes.

There's Thad . . . but how is that remotely my fault?

Finally, there's Mitch. He's in some sort of gray category I can't name. He seemed so perfect and then suddenly—not. His behavior has certainly not been consistent. And he is secretive, that text message rising up to remind me that he isn't a good choice.

Boel drags me back to the moment with, "At the Seattle Pacific Ballet Company . . . we pride ourselves on our professionalism."

*Seriously?*

He ignores my stance, which clearly says, *Back off.* My leotard begins to stick to my body as it chills against my skin.

"Miss Mackey . . . ," he says, and something about the way he says it makes my body still. "I'm going to break protocol this one time, so you must listen."

I wait, my heart thumping uncomfortably in my chest.

"You have a gift." He casts his eyes down, his face reddening slightly, and I almost laugh; his discomfort is so acute I can smell it. Mr. Give the Criticisms Out Like Candy is choking on his words.

He looks back at me, his gaze locking with mine. "I will use a cliché: you were born to dance." He ditches any pretense of composure, stepping forward, and I hold my ground as he enters my personal space, our bodies kissing close. "There, I've said it. Do not let this strange thing that follows you rob the world of seeing what you have been given. Do not."

Boel doesn't touch me but his words do. They drill into my soul. He's put me on notice without saying. His hands are tied. Boel will let me go if there is another occurrence of the kind of thing that happened with Brock.

Or closet sex, I'm pretty sure.

Because the Seattle Pacific Ballet Company is beyond reproach. They don't have *principals* who are attacked by serial killers. Or . . . who have sex in odd places.

"Are we clear, Miss Mackey?" His eyes stare into mine, never wavering.

I let a heartbeat go . . . two. "Crystal."

"Excellent," he says, and spins as he moves away, a dancer's move. Also an evasive one.

I'm moping in my room, having heard nothing from Cas for five days.

Carlie saves me from languishing another weekend in my room.

"Come on, Mackey!"

"I don't want to, it's embarrassing . . ."

Sympathy flashes across her face, then is gone. "You can't hide from the curious forever."

*Yeah I can.* I'll be the girl who escaped the serial killer forever.

"Let's go get the mani/pedi thing done!" Amber yells into the close confines of my room, and I wince.

I don't think I want my feet seen or pampered. They'll just be beaten into submission again with Boel on Monday.

"We're going, no arguments!" Amber says, and I follow behind like a beaten puppy. I have a shift at Java Head tomorrow and another weekend thinking about, you guessed it, Devin Castile.

Carlie drives and I'm quiet, thinking about all the threats in my life. It's better without Cas. He's nothing but trouble.

The lie I tell myself doesn't stop my body from mourning him with a profound grief. It aches for his touch and all the things his beautiful parts do to me, for me. My heart does too. Bruised and needy. It's like that hiatus in hiding doubled up on me when I got a taste of what I've been missing, and I'm almost less happy having had it. Before, I had nothing to miss.

Now I know.

"Hey, ya downer . . . we're gonna get you beautiful!" Amber says as we pull up to the mall to get buffed and polished.

"Miss him, huh?" Carlie asks, seeing through all my shit.

I blow a wisp of hair out of my eyes and it floats back down against my cheek. "Yeah," I say, breathy.

"Fuck men," Amber says loyally.

"Yeah, fuck men," Carlie says with a dreamy voice. "Big, muscly, get-me-some abs . . . kinda men."

I laugh; I can't help it. She always knows how to make me lighter than I am.

We traipse into the mall and choose the first nail salon we come across.

FANCY NAILS, the sign claims. Uh-huh.

We sit down and strip our winter boots and socks off.

"I make your feet look pretty," an Asian pedicurist promises.

But he hasn't seen my feet . . . really *looked*.

Though anything would be better than what's going on now. He looks at my beaten feet and asks, "What do you do to your feet, pretty girl?"

"I dance," I answer.

"You pay extra for more work." His syllables pop like second-language gunfire.

"Okay." I relent and Carlie shrieks laughter beside me.

"I love you long time," she giggles while she shakes her ample bosom back and forth and my face flames in embarrassment.

He scowls at Carlie and so the abuse on my feet begins, but I groan with pleasure when he puts them in the hot bath with the lavender crystals.

"Girl, your feet look like shit," Amber says, gazing at the bunions and blisters now buried in a sudsy warm bath.

Carlie motions to Amber to come nearer and Amber leans over the armrest of the pedi chair, the rhythm of the massager beating against her back and making her tremble while she sits. "Secret," Carlie says.

"Do tell," Amber says.

"Men don't fuck feet," she says, deadpan, and I laugh.

"Thank God for small favors," I say as the male pedicurist glares at the three of us equally.

I wink at Carlie and Amber smiles.

I've begun to live in the moment without realizing it.

# SIXTEEN

~

*T*he text comes in at a moment when I'm not thinking about Cas at all.

*Hey babe.*

"*Hey babe*"? I blow my hair out of my eyes in a huff. He doesn't text me for almost a week after I get my head thrown against a wall and then it's "*Hey babe*"?

I walk down the sidewalk as it weaves away from the parking lot after Carlie drops me off. I can feel my toe shoes I had left in her car over the weekend softly bounce on my back, the laces tied and held over my shoulder like a purse handle.

*How do I answer?* I get a deep twinge of excitement inside and hold my thumb over the *reply* symbol, hesitating. The next text reads:

*Stop being indecisive and text back.*

I jump like Cas is standing right there. Giving a furtive look around and seeing no one, I laugh a little at how stupid

I'm acting. *So sue me,* I think, fuming at myself. After Mitch treating me like a turd and the thing with Brock . . . I'm a little blown away lately.

*Hey,* I text back noncommittally. My hand trembles as I tap *reply.*

I suck my lip inside my mouth, smoothly rolling it inside and out. My nervousness is alive and kicking again, the butterflies fluttering toward escape. But I'm not going to open the lid just yet. I'm done with people pushing me around.

I'm bone tired of hiding.

*I have a surprise for you.*

The butterflies spring free, caressing my entire body from the inside out. They float, searching for release, for freedom.

My breaths come rapidly and my heart speeds.

*What?* I text, stopping.

*You'll see,* is the cryptic reply.

My mind does a replay of the closet and I feel my body tighten down low, the blood rushing to my sex. From his text alone. Those innocent words can mean anything, I reason.

But I know better. Nothing about Cas is innocent.

I begin walking again, then I break into a jog.

My feet fly, my slippers a flag of faded pink satin behind me as I hit the door at breakneck speed. I take the steps two at a time to reach the second level and burst into my room, barely out of breath. I am an elite athlete and the little sprint doesn't cause my heart to stutter.

Cas does.

And all of him is inside my room and waiting. The heart

conditioned for dance breaks and runs like an escaped horse at
the races. Racing, racing . . . quaking.

Then he's wrapping me against him. The smell of him hits
me: mint, leather, male and the faint scent of tobacco. The smell
of Cas.

"You should get that knob fixed, Jess," he says in soft reprimand, walking me toward the wall, my feet on top of his own.

"You shouldn't be waiting in my room like a stalker," I say.

He lets a slow smile spread over his face, his deep eyes lighting from within, sucking me down into the ebony depths.

He pushes me against my wall with his hips.

"Don't," I say, pushing at him.

He puts his hands on either side of my face and whispers,
"Don't what?"

"Don't play me," I say, honest for the first time, making my
needs known . . . in actual words.

He frowns and his beautiful teeth flash in the darkness of my
room. Cas trails a finger from my temple to my jawbone. "Beautiful Jess, my dancer . . ." He lays a hot kiss beside my eye; I feel
his lashes flutter against my own and I sigh despite my resolve.

"Trust me a little while longer and then I'll let you in on my
secret." He gives me a level look and I stare back.

"How can I trust you? You don't text me for days, then when
you see me it's all about sex."

Cas cocks a brow. "You said *only* sex . . ." He trails off but
there's a look in his face, and just as I think I'm understanding
what it means he flicks his eyes away. Like he knew he would
give something away.

But what?

I curl my hand around the nape of his muscular neck and he buries his hand at the small of my back, his mouth going to my throat. I spear my fingers in his short hair, which is just past a buzz cut, and the soft hair gives under the clench of my fingers. I grip him hard and pull; he shudders under my touch. "Don't do that, vanilla girl."

"Or what?" I ask breathlessly.

And he shows me. Cas hikes me against the wall. "You said just fucking, Jess."

He grinds his hips against my lower body, his engorged cock splitting my lips apart, and I gasp as an electric surge floods my system, beginning at my sex and spreading like a wildfire ignited. My hips give a responding swivel.

"Ah . . . Jess," he breathes out, pressing his cock against me. He covers my throat with one hand and squeezes as he dry-humps me in a deliberate slow circle against the wall.

"Tell me it's just fucking," he says in a low growl, working his dick against me with a delicious friction that plays havoc with my resolve. My legs dangle on either side of his hips. One strong hand grips my ass and the other pins me by my throat. The mix of tender and brutal maneuvers makes my sex grow wet and swollen, his cock never wavering in its assault on my neediness.

"Tell me," he says, wringing it out of me with his steady rhythm. I want him beating that staccato rhythm of the ages deep inside me.

"It's not just sex." I whisper the truth into the room as his panting breath and gyrations get faster and harder, my back sliding up and down against the wall.

"Tell me!" he orders, and I scream around the fingers that hold me fast against the wall.

"It's not just sex!" I yell in a hoarse shout that can be heard from down the dorm hall.

He slowly lets me down, his cock a stiff rod inside his pants, my tears a heated stream on my face.

"I know it isn't," he says in a voice full of emotion.

"What is it, then, Cas . . . ?" I grab the front of his black T-shirt and grip it in my fist. He doesn't move with the force of my pull, though I put my body weight into it.

"It's something we can't do. Not right now."

I feel like someone's punched me. I back away and he watches me, those dark eyes following me like a hawk spying prey.

"So what? *You bastard,*" I say, my voice breaking. "If you knew it had . . . become more, why couldn't you just let. Me. Go?"

He rakes a hand through his short hair, his gaze traveling my body so slowly it seems little more than a steady stare until I notice those eyes, shining in the dark velvet of my room.

When his eyes reach my face, he sighs. "Because I can't. I never could."

"Do you care for me?" I ask, my heart in my voice, my arms shaking, the tears collecting like wet heat in the hollows of my collarbone.

*I don't want a relationship; it's dangerous.*

"Not in the way you think," he replies. And I hear the truth ringing in his voice.

I realize in that moment that all I want is to be with Cas.

I'm so hurt I can't breathe. He "surprises" me by giving me the best foreplay in the world, then basically dumps me.

"Get out," I manage to croak as he moves toward me.

"Jess . . . ," he says, and reaches out to touch me. I flinch away when my body is screaming for his hands on me.

"No," I say, holding up my hand. "We're so unhealthy." My watery eyes look into his and they tighten with whatever they see there. "You thought you'd come by and fuck me and make it all better. Well you're not even a fuck buddy, Cas . . . you're . . . I don't know, worse than a user."

His face hardens in anger. "It's not what you think, Jess."

I put my fist on my hip, my other hand gripping the side of the door. "Then you tell me what the fuck it is, Cas! Tell me right now or go," I yell, uncaring about the warning Boel gave me, my dorm mates hearing or anything else resembling the rational.

He shakes his head regretfully and before I can say anything he crushes me against him, his hand buried into the thick knot of my hair, and he presses his mouth against mine, bruising my lips until I open them for him. I do because I want him—even with how he's treated me, *I want him.*

But in the end it's Cas who lets me go.

He tears himself from me, his chest heaving, the cords in his neck standing out. "When you know everything, then none of this will matter," he says, making no sense.

"It will matter," I say, pointing to the hall, where several students have peeked out in various stages of dress, and upon seeing a dangerous-looking man step out of my room, they quickly shut their doors.

He turns to say something and I slam the door in his face.

It's a self-protective measure so I don't fling myself in his arms.

My doorknob comes off, falling to the floor with a clunk, and I kick it across the room, hurting my newly polished toes in the process.

I throw myself on my bed and cry, the pieces of whatever heart I have left splintering apart and drifting away on the sea of my sorrow.

⁓

Have you ever been so sad, cried so much, that your eyelids were at half mast? Well I have, and mine are. I walk the corridors of anonymity at the U Dub on Monday, my head bent, my sore eyes so itchy and tender I want to cry again because of it.

*Damn him.*

*Damn me,* I think, and give a little smile of self-insult.

I make slow progress in the cafeteria line, the lunch lady taking one look at my face and patting my hand as she puts everything that is white on my tray.

Comfort food central.

I shove the mounded tray on the table and begin eating the pound cake first.

"Damn!" Carlie says as she watches my devouring of the dessert as an appetizer. Then she catches sight of my face and lowers herself slowly to sit on the bench beside me.

"What happened?" she asks softly.

"He dumped me," I say, because it's how I see it.

"No!" she hisses in disbelief. Then she frowns. "I thought it was just sex."

I dump the pound cake on the tray and it falls over and rolls to a stop on the plastic lip.

I shake my head, my eyelids burning. "I . . . it's not."

"You're not hardwired that way, Mackey."

I swallow my grief with the pound cake, washing it down with a swig of cold milk straight out of the carton. "Oh yeah?" I await Carlie's revelation.

"Remember that creepy old movie *The Silence of the Lambs*?"

I'm puzzled out of my momentary wallowing. "What . . . ah, yeah; Jodie Foster."

She points her finger at me. "That's the one." She looks up at the ceiling, remembering. "Well remember when Anthony Hopkins—"

There is a clatter as someone empties their lunch into the trash bin and I ask a little louder over the din, "Who?"

"Hannibal the Cannibal."

I make a face—*yuck*. The serial killer reference is a little too close to home. "Yeah," I answer.

"When he talked about the deep roller and the shallow rollers?"

"Yes," I say, my interest piqued. "The pigeons," I add.

Her look nails me to my seat. "You're a deep roller, Mackey."

I look at her, thinking that I've just been compared to a pigeon. The ungainly birds that annoy everyone and shit all over the place.

Amber slides in across from us. "Who's a deep roller?" Her

brows cock above her light golden eyes as she truncates a carrot with her practiced mouth.

I smile a little.

"Mackey here is."

"*The Silence of the Lambs*," Amber says, using the carrot end to swirl ranch dressing.

I roll my eyes at them. *With the movies!*

"I don't believe what Hannibal said about how a shallow roller shouldn't mate with a deep roller," Carlie says.

Amber nods. With her mouth full, she talks behind her cupped hand. "Carlie's right."

"Huh?" I ask, looking between the two of them.

"I think"—Carlie pauses for dramatic effect—"that a deep roller protects another like themselves."

"Well, that *is* . . . deep, for you," I say, winking.

"Hey!" She bats me in my arm and I give a yelp. "I'm not that shallow, I consider shit."

Amber and I look at her.

She relents. "Some shit. Anyway, I think Castile's a deep roller, Jess."

"Ooh la la . . . Cas," Amber says, chiming in.

"Shut up, he just dumped her."

"I thought it was just sex," Amber states, biting off another carrot.

I groan and my face plunges into my hands, my eyes begging for a good mindless rubbing.

"All I'm saying, Jess, is: Cas is a deep roller and he's gonna come back and want to mate with another deep roller."

"That's not healthy," Amber says. "Two deep rollers are supposed to be bad together."

"Yeah," I say, trying to convince myself not to care.

Carlie shakes her head. "I think they move toward each other, like magnets. They can't help it." Her hands come together with a smack, the fingers lacing together tightly.

"Sounds messed up, intense . . . dysfunctional," Amber says, picking up a crumb of my forgotten pound cake and popping it into her mouth.

"It is," Carlie says in agreement. "But who ever said that love makes sense? That it's healthy . . . that it's *right*? Love is inexplicable," Carlie says, and I look at her in surprise.

She gives a snort. "I'm not just another pretty face. I got a near-perfect score on my SATs, Miss Smarty Panties."

"Golden panties," I say, correcting her.

Amber guffaws. "I heard about the closet . . . ," she says.

*Gawd, will I ever be able to get past that?*

"I think it's hot," she says in a dreamy voice.

"What about Mitch?" I ask Carlie, ignoring Amber's musings about my indiscretions.

"As a pigeon?"

"He's a dick, I hear," Amber announces casually.

I scowl, seeking my flighty friend's innate wisdom. She takes my question seriously but answers far quicker than I'd like.

"Shallow for sure," she says with slow deliberation.

"How do you know?" I ask.

"The eyes." Carlie gives a slight quiver of her shoulders. "I thought he was La Hunk but he's La Creeper."

Amber stops digging through my lunch tray and puts my tapioca pudding down with a clunk, the spoon falling out and the seedy goop splattering slightly on the bright orange plastic.

I think of those pale eyes in my mind, how warm they were at my audition, how he kissed me so tenderly. As time wore on, it seemed he was moving almost methodically toward some goal I was unaware of.

Maybe I'm imagining things.

Speak of the devil; Mitch walks up to the table. His pale eyes are as I remember them.

Doesn't matter. I stand, ignoring him, and begin to pick up my tray. If he came to gloat because Cas has ditched me, because even our sex wasn't enough to keep Devin Castile's interest and a relationship made him dread me . . . Well, I'm not going to have Mitch rub it in and tell me what he thinks of my behavior.

Salt in the fucking wound I don't need.

"I'm sorry," he says. It stops me in my tracks and I see Carlie pull her head back with a weird look, like, *WTF?*

"How sorry?" Carlie asks, leaning forward.

He laughs a little, color rising in his face. He clears his throat, swinging his dark hair out of his eyes and staring into mine. "Very."

Mitch looks at Amber and Carlie, then swings those beautiful gray eyes to mine, and they're filled with cautious hope. "Can we talk, Jess?"

I sigh. I can't tell him no, but it doesn't mean it'll ever be yes either.

"Yeah," I say, giving a little wave to Carlie.

"You text me if you need me," Carlie says, narrowing her gaze on Mitch.

"I'm watching you," she tells Mitch, and he looks at Carlie, their gazes locking for a moment. Then the hardness leaves his expression and it softens when he looks back at me.

He takes my backpack and we walk out into the hall, finally making our way outside. Thankfully, he doesn't take me to the same spot where he basically called me a slut.

I cross my arms, my charity only stretching so far.

"Okay, I'm here, Mitch."

"I'd just found out about Brock, Jess." He casts a glance around him, then speaks into the light breeze that has sprung up, and I shiver. We're a day away from Christmas break and it's pretty cold. Of course, tomorrow it could be a balmy fifty-five degrees. Welcome to Seattle.

"And the guys were talking about how you were banging Castile, and Brock . . . he killed Tawny," he says, his fists clenching.

"Your lacrosse teammates were speculating about what happened in the closet with *us* rather than the serial killer being *caught*?" I scoff, beginning to move away. I don't need a recounting of what happened in the closet; I know. I'm not forgetting that slice of the hottest sex ever any time soon, broken heart or not.

"Yeah . . . no!" he says loudly, raking his dark hair back, the fall of his bangs sweeping into his face again. "It's all part of it. They don't know that Tawny was my sister—different last names, y'know."

*Right,* of course.

"I just saw red. They'd finally caught the bastard and they said you and Cas were all wrapped up in what happened and to know that . . . that he'd had you like some whore in that room . . ." He cast his eyes down to his feet while I blushed to the roots of my hair.

It wouldn't be so bad if Cas backed me. If he were with me now. But he isn't. He was all secretive and wanting to have sex with me when it worked for him. Now he doesn't even want that.

"I'm not a whore," I say so softly I figure he doesn't hear me.

I swipe at my swollen lids as they begin to leak again.

"Jesus, Jess . . . I know. Come here," he says, pulling me against him, and I cry against his chest, the pieces of my soaked heart flowing away with the river of my sadness, drenching his shirt, drowning my soul.

"Shh . . . ," he murmurs, stroking my hair.

"Get your fucking hands off her," Cas says from somewhere behind us.

I don't even turn. I'm wrung out.

"Why don't you ask Jess what she wants, Devin?" Mitch asks, using his name like a curse word.

Cas circles us and I press my face against Mitch's chest. I can't face Cas; it's too raw, his rejection of me a fresh seeping wound.

"Well?" Mitch says. "*Ask her*, Castile."

"Jess," Cas says with a husky catch in his voice.

Just his voice makes my body react. Does he even know how dangerous he is? *Do I?*

*Yes.*

"Go away, Devin," I say, using his real name.

"Look at me. Tell me you want Mitch and I'll go," he says.

I look at him from the circle of Mitch's arms and it's a mistake. His brooding eyes are on me like banked fire, the muscles of his body taut with unease and expectation, his dark, short hair like an inky cap.

"I don't want you," I lie through my teeth.

"You're lying," he says.

*So true.*

"You heard her," Mitch says, holding me against him.

My eyes flick to Cas, then away.

I don't like what I see there. It doesn't look like what he's told me.

His words said he doesn't want me.

But his body loved mine, it did. I felt the flames of his feelings consuming me.

Right now, his eyes say he loves me.

*I can't do it.*

Whatever it is with Cas, *I can't.*

"I want Mitch," I say.

The second lie of the night.

Devin Castile stares at me for a moment, then he turns on his heel and walks away.

He doesn't look back.

I can't look away.

# SEVENTEEN

〜

$\mathcal{M}$itch walks me to my next class and the tears don't come. Neither does anything else. It's like my feelings have been stolen. I hang on to the idea of dance at four o'clock today like an anchor. That will be the one time where I don't think about Cas, my hidden life, the mess with Mitch . . . I can just let the dance take me.

"I'll text you later, 'kay?" Mitch asks, his hand holding mine, his gray eyes sweeping over my features, searching for an emotion, anything. I'm sure he's discovered what I already know: an insidious indifference has taken up residence where my passion was. Like ink slipping out of a bottle, it slides toward the lowest grade. I can feel the black spreading inside me.

"Jess?" Mitch repeats softly.

"Huh?" I ask, then quickly nod my head and answer, "Sure."

"Great," Mitch says, and leans down to peck my cheek, and

I let him, my mind shying away from the boiling image of Cas inside my brain.

~

The day drones on; the other students have stopped staring at me every moment of every day. I can actually move through the halls without a path of eyeballs sinking into my back as I go by. It's good because today I desperately need anonymity again.

I trudge up the stairs and toe my door open, and the ineffective doorknob I shoved back in place rattles. I stare at the thing after slamming the door closed with my hip. It hangs at an angle, mocking me.

I frown. The hell with it; this weekend I'll get Carlie to take me to the hardware store and I'll install a new one myself.

I begin my warm-ups at the barre; I hate arriving cold for Boel. Big mistake. When my body begins to heat my leotard and tights and I'm almost sweating, I chance a glance at the clock on my nightstand. The glaring blue digital numbers say 3:44; time to go. I rush out the door and hear the knob engage the striker, and, satisfied it's secure enough after having twisted the internal lock while in the room, I jam my keys in my duffel and fly down the stairs toward dance practice.

The knob drops from the flimsy brass cradle again and hits the floor, rolling underneath my bed.

I never see it because I'm halfway to the auditorium by that time; I only put it together after.

Of course, I mistakenly created a situation that encourages a predator to attack.

Opportunity.

~

Boel is his normal, consistent self, pressing Shelby and me to our limits, then past them.

"He's gonna kill us," Shelby says in a whisper as she lands next to me.

"Again!" Boel roars, cracking his palms together, and we make our diagonal progress across the auditorium. My head whips, finding my corner as my leg bends rhythmically to allow as many pirouettes as humanly possible before I reach the other corner.

I hear the clap of Boel's hands as he counts with his body and his mind. How many times can I spin with perfect form in the space allotted?

*Quite a few,* I decide as I make a gliding landing into third position. Boel strides to Shelby and I hold third. I hear a grunt behind me and know Boel will strike in the next second. He does, grasping my thigh, and it's solid, unmovable.

I turn and he gives a rare smile. I grin back like a fool.

"You've done well, Miss Mackey."

It's the second compliment he's given me in all the time we've been practicing.

"You may go, both of you."

Shelby shrugs and I walk away, glancing back once to see

Boel, his arms crossed over his lean and muscular chest. The ghost of a smile rides his lips.

⌒

"Come on, Jess," Shelby says.

I never make new friends. I already botched it big-time with Carlie and to a lesser extent, Amber. If only I could have committed myself to a friendless existence that secured my anonymity. I can't . . . I won't.

But today was kick-ass and I'm riding that high. *Boel said I did well.* Even with Cas not into me . . . his running around wearing my heart on his sleeve like a trophy, I can't be totally sad.

I feel the corner of my lips twitch. "Okay, yeah."

We're freshly scrubbed and I give my ballet outfit a sniff and chuck it right into my locker. I hesitate over my slippers, bending and straightening them by habit.

"What?" Shelby asks, her dark brows popping, halting my nervous fidget.

I don't want to leave my slippers. My pointe shoes have an almost talismanic relationship with me. If I have them in my possession, good things happen. I sigh, realizing I'm being foolish.

*Stupid superstition.* I put them carefully on top of my ballet gear. I don't throw them.

Not so silly after all, as the slippers will inadvertently save my life.

At the last moment, I pick them up, placing them with

Shelby's. There, she has a locker whose combo works; mine has never locked properly.

"Let's go, ballerina," she says, looping her arm through mine.

"You're a dancer too," I say in protest as we march down the hall, my jeans dragging a little over the heels of my Dansko clogs.

Shelby nods. "I know, Jess . . . but you're gonna be principal."

I open my mouth to protest and she shushes me. "Listen, I have eyes in my head. I see the way Boel looks at you . . ."

I turn, looking at her as her hand rests on the bar of the door leading out to the parking lot, a hot breve waiting for me at the coffeehouse of her choice.

"How does he look at me?" I ask, because I don't know. I'm too busy spinning and leaping to catch the emotional signature of Boel.

"Like he just won the lottery," she says.

"Oh," I say softly.

"Isn't that what you wanted?" Shelby asks, her eyes searching mine.

*I always end up as somebody's prize.* "Yeah, I guess."

Shelby rolls her eyes. "You're crazy . . ."

*Maybe.*

We walk out into the night together.

Malevolence hangs just out of reach, waiting for its companion, opportunity.

"So we never talk," Shelby says, warming her hands on the sleeveless stiff coffee cup.

I do the same and smile at her. "No, we don't. We're too busy getting our asses handed to us by Boel."

Shelby gives a sarcastic snort, trying not to spit her coffee out. "That's the God's honest truth."

We tap our coffee cups together. "Damn straight."

Shelby drags her finger in circles around the lip of her cup, her eyes flicking to mine. "What do you think his problem is?"

I feel my brows rise. "Boel? He doesn't have a problem. He's all about the ballet."

"*The* ballet . . . ," Shelby muses out loud.

I nod, taking a small sip of the creamy confection of my breve, loving the taste.

"You got a guy?" she asks.

I look at her and she registers some information from my expression.

"Noooo . . . ," she breathes, her eyes becoming wide.

"Yeah," I say, my eyes glued to my cooling coffee.

"He's like . . . *hot*," she says.

*Gee, thanks,* I think. "Well, we're not seeing each other anymore," I say in answer, lifting a shoulder and letting it drop.

"God, girl . . . why not?"

My eyes meet hers. Shelby whistles low in her throat, leaning back. "You got it bad."

I don't deny it.

Shelby's hand covers mine. "It'll be okay." She pats my hand.

I don't feel like it'll be. Ever. In fact, I feel vaguely ill.

"We'll dance it out," she says sagely.

"Huh?" I ask, sipping my coffee. I set it down; it's grown

a little too cold to enjoy. I'm a transplant to Seattle; I'd never drink it cold or old like a local.

"We'll dance until you can't think about Stud Muffin."

"Okaaay . . . ," I say slowly. "Where?"

"Skoochie's."

"No way, he bounces there," I say.

Shelby rolls her eyes, giving my outfit a once-over. "I guess you'll do."

"No," I say.

Her eyes narrow and an evil sparkle glimmers in them. "Oh yes. We'll dance it out in front of Castile."

I widen my eyes.

She nods. "I never forget a hot-looking guy . . ."

I laugh. "How does that work out?"

Shelby laughs too. "Not too great so far, but hope springs eternal, they say."

I think about that for a minute. "Who the hell is 'they,' anyway?"

Shelby shrugs, wrapping her scarf around her throat. "A bunch of assholes in dark, windowless rooms, thinking up expressions that sound good in theory."

I stand. "That's what I thought."

"Let's go and show Stud who's boss."

*Maybe Cas won't be working.*

No. Such. Luck.

Shelby has the bottomless purse and does my face up in her car outside the Starbucks.

"Sit still, open your mouth wider," Shelby instructs, her full lower lip held tightly between her teeth. She takes her time, having already applied eye shadow and liner and swiped mascara on each of my lashes.

I look in the rearview mirror and don't recognize myself; I'm all cheekbones and eyes. Blue ones, my natural green still safely hidden away underneath the contacts.

Shelby eyes me critically. "We're the same size . . ." She digs through a second bag, pulling out spiky heels and a gauzy top in a shimmering aqua.

It will barely cover my boobs.

"No," I say, giving her the sign of the vampire cross, my index fingers crossed over each other.

"Do you want him to notice you?"

*Yes.* "Not really."

"Liar," Shelby says, and I don't refute her.

Again.

I change quickly and she gets a twin outfit to mine. Her shoes are a little snug.

"How tall are you?" I ask.

"Five four," she answers.

*That's why my feet are cramped.*

"Tight?" she asks, eying the borrowed stilettos.

I nod.

Another shrug. "Beauty is pain."

*Right.* Or pain is just pain.

Shelby scoots into the driver's seat, closing her compact

with a snap. She pulls out of the university parking lot and we head to Skoochie's.

My stomach's in my throat.

I've become the thing I detest, a player. It isn't my style. None of this is.

I guess I'm making one last attempt at exhausting this thing between me and Cas. Just thinking about him put the familiar ache between my legs. The longing to have him here swept reason out of my mind like errant cobwebs from a corner.

Another crowd waits and I rise up on my toes to see if Cas is there.

I hate to admit I'm a little disappointed when he isn't.

"You see him?" Shelby asks, looking herself.

I shake my head.

"That's okay, you still look good enough to eat," she says, winking. An image of Cas's tongue as he licks my lips and plunges that hot wetness inside me rises unbidden in my mind and I actually stop breathing for a second.

Our attraction is so lethal, so completely overwhelming, it doesn't feel real. I can always talk myself out of the animal magnetism when he's not around. When he's there, it's all too real. I give a hard swallow, moving farther up in the line. I recognize the other bouncer that Cas helped a couple of weeks ago. It seems like a lifetime ago now.

He gives me a once-over, flicking his eyes to Shelby. "You two, go." He jerks his chin at the entrance door and moves aside.

The music hits us with an almost physical blow, a wall of noise like a tidal wave of water, inundating us with its low, primal beat, the strobe and multicolored lights casting puzzle pieces like fallen jewels on our faces, bare arms and breasts, which are offered like ripe fruit within the confines of our skimpy tops.

Who says ballet dancers cannot dance? We can; we do. Shelby and I pick up a rhythm that is all our own, effortlessly transitioning from ballet to the fast gyration necessary to keep up with the thumping beat the club is pumping out. Like girls do, we dance with each other.

My eyes are closed, my arms and legs moving to the beat, my hips swiveling in perfect tandem with my limbs. When strong arms come around me it seems like the missing heat that I need. That I've always needed.

He moves like he is meant to be against my body, pressed up against me. Riding me.

*I know.*

I turn in his arms and Cas presses me against him, hip to chin, marrying our bodies just as surely as if he were inside me. The clothes keep us apart only because they cover our bodies. If they didn't, I can't say he wouldn't act on that earth-shattering chemistry that engulfs us when we are together, as it does now.

"No," I say against him, his steady heartbeat thudding against my cheek. It's too loud to hear but he says, "Yes."

I tear away from him and I can feel him follow me. As I push through the bodies my eyes scan the crowd for Shelby.

She catches sight of me and her eyes go round when she sees the freight train that is Cas up my ass.

*How did I ever think we wouldn't come together like magnets if we were in the same vicinity?* It was ten different types of stupid. But that's sort of normal for me when it comes to Cas.

"Hey!" Shelby yells, interposing her body between Cas's and mine.

He ignores her, grabbing my arm smoothly from around her body, and swings me to him.

He grabs both my arms and without preamble slams his lips on mine.

I twine my arms around his strong neck and I can feel the rumble of a groan vibrate through our smashed bodies.

"Way to play it cool, Jess!" Shelby yells.

It brings me down to earth one shattering syllable at a time. Quiet descends for three seconds before the next song begins. Cas's face rises above me like a dark moon, the lights from the strobe flashing jagged colors across his cheekbones, strange colors artificially lighting his eyes, then falling away to blackness again.

I turn and feel our fingers taper off, then fall away. Shelby takes my hand, which was just on Cas's flesh. She tows me behind her, making a getaway for the back entrance of Skoochies.

I look over my shoulder and Cas is coming, his hands in fists, his body a taut line of intensity, all of it focused on me.

We stumble outside, among a bunch of people in various stages of dress. Smoking, drinking . . . and some making out . . . and more.

I whirl and Cas is there. "Don't talk, Jess," he says.

"No," I say in a low voice. "We don't do enough of that. Has something changed? Are you ready to tell me your secret?" I ask.

Silence.

The only noise is the people milling around us on a night too cold to be outside without a jacket. My skin pebbles in response to the cool air that licks it.

Or maybe it's from being that close to Castile.

"Forget it, Jess," Shelby says, her gaze landing on Cas with disdain. "He's not worth it. Kinda outta control if you ask me."

His dark eyes shift to her and whatever she sees there causes her to take a step back. "I didn't. Ask. You."

"Come on, Jess. Let's go get drunk or something . . . ," Shelby says.

*Bad ballerina, bad.*

"Okay," I say, not meaning it. But in the gloom of the outside, a busted pair of streetlights all the light there is, Cas can't tell the lie from the truth.

"No . . . *Jess.* Don't go off half-cocked. I know it's my fault . . ."

I turn on him. "You got that right."

Then I walk off. The tap of my heels as I catch up with Shelby sounds like gunfire in the parking lot, amplified by my anger.

I slide into the car, slamming my hand on the door lock, and look toward Cas.

Where he was.

Where he isn't any longer.

I turn away seething as Shelby pulls out.

We were at Skoochie's for an hour and it felt like a hundred years. I can still feel his skin against mine; my lips are plump from his kisses, my panties hot and moist from the arousal brought on by his nearness. From a kiss and half a dance. I let my hand drop from my bruised mouth and stifle a moan of defeat.

"That didn't go well," Shelby says, the streetlights hitting her face every few seconds.

"No," I whisper.

"I didn't know, Jess, I'm sorry . . . he . . ."

"I can't be without him." I swipe at my leaking eyes again and want to take them out with a spoon.

"You can't be with him," she says, stepping on the gas.

"Exactly," I say in agreement, slumping in my seat, the borrowed outfit clinging to me like a costume.

I'm so tired of hiding underneath stuff: clothing, contacts, hair color. My personality.

Cas saw through that, like an arrow through my heart; *he saw me.*

Jewell MacLeod.

# EIGHTEEN

～

"*He is hot*, Jess," Shelby mumbles as we walk to my dorm room. I tap in the entry code on the keypad and the door buzzes. We scoot inside and the door rattles closed.

"Where the hell is everyone in your dorm?" she asks.

I look around at the empty hall and shrug. "I have a wing where there's no shares."

"No shit." she says, looking around like it's the best thing ever. No shares simply means less people, a good thing for my needs of staying hidden.

I barely keep up on the payments. It's actually an experiment for the university to see if closets can be dorm rooms. Apparently, *yes*, they can. Who knew?

We begin hoofing it up the stairs. "At least you don't have to worry about security anymore with that douche Brock put away."

I swallow the lump in my throat and she puts her hand on my back. It lets me know that she won't talk about it until I'm ready.

I don't know when that will be, but not for the reasons she's probably thinking.

"Cuz this building is not secure, just sayin' . . ."

We get to the top of my hall and I look around. I guess I haven't noticed; it's always hide, separate, survive. Less people seems like a benie. Now it somehow seems sinister, the lack of bodies allowing a lot of things to go unnoticed.

Now it's screw Cas, evade Cas, pine for Cas.

Not necessarily in that order.

We stop in front of my door, my hand on my keys. *Damn it.* I left my stinky gear back at the locker. I look over my shoulder and Shelby catches me looking at the door, then at my empty hands.

"Forget it, you have extras, right?" she asks, instantly re-membering my ditched gear and putting it together.

I do, but God, they'll reek.

"It was sorta worth it?" she asks.

"It proved that I am screwed is what it did." I give a sad little chuckle and she squeezes my arm.

"It's okay, it'll work out and it was good to have coffee and get gussied up."

I smile, then I see her frown.

"He likes you, Jess."

"He likes this," I say, pointing to my golden kitty.

Shelby smirks. "Yeah, I totally got that he liked that . . . but you didn't see his eyes."

I wait.

"He *really* likes you, Jess," Shelby says.

I turn away, key ready to open the door, and reply, "When he figures out being honest with me, then maybe—"

The doorknob is gone.

It's like someone put me in quicksand, but I'm treading instead of sinking, held stationary. I watch Shelby's mouth open and ask what's wrong. I understand that's what she's saying but I don't hear her because the door has swung inward.

Thaddeus MacLeod is standing in the middle of the room.

"Hello, sister," he says, moving like striking lighting.

I turn and the first useful thing I've said escapes my mouth. "Run!" I scream at Shelby. Her arms pinwheel, her mind undecided: should she run as told or stay and help? Her thought process is so transparent it would be funny if my serial-killer brother weren't in the room.

I could tell her there is no protection from Thad. If he's here, we're as good as dead. It isn't a complicated concept.

His hands land on me and that familiar rolling nausea begins in my stomach with a chaser of hot dread.

I swing my face around and see Mitch; relief floods my system.

"Get that bitch before she makes noise," I hear Thad tell Mitch, and something dies inside me when he spares me a brief glance.

His smile never reaches his eyes. Those unnerving eyes sweep over my imprisoned body and then he is after Shelby. She's fast, I can hear her footsteps as she runs, his pounding after hers.

I listen to them down the hall from where I stand in my room when Mitch catches up to Shelby.

She never stood a chance, and the blood roars in my ears like a river of fear, capsizing me inside the gray waters of my mind, the black eating the edges like the caps on top of the water as they drive higher.

Mitch enters the room as quietly as he left, carrying an unconscious and bleeding Shelby over his shoulder.

The emotional roar inside me has no bounds; my betrayal and misery are so acute I can hardly breathe.

"Make it fast, I want to get my darling sibling out of here and somewhere quiet."

Mitch dumps Shelby on the floor like a box of rocks and her head cracks against the wood. I flinch as it gives a soft echo, almost as if the wood is distressed by the impact. He turns at the waist, scooping up a round implement, covered by a blanket.

My favorite quilt.

I watch the jagged pattern of squares rise and fall on Shelby.

I can't make out the design for the blood, as it is raised over and over again above Mitch's head like an evil baton, the white becoming red.

I sag against Thad, my vision trembling as the black hovers like great wings, ready to take me.

"Do it," I hear Thad say to Mitch.

Those pale eyes light on me like a cool fire.

Then he swings the instrument of death at me.

Pain explodes inside my knee and Thad covers my mouth as I shriek my agony into his hand. Vomit rises and I begin to choke on my puke; the pain of my knee is beyond screaming. I retch against his hand while the gore of Shelby lies at my feet.

I let the blackness take me.

But before the waters of my mind put me under, Thad whispers in my ear, "No more dancing for you . . ."

And I know no more.

### Castile

Cas watched the woman who had rocked his world leave the dance club that was part of his carefully constructed deception. Lowering his chin to the sensitive mic, he relayed the information: "Subject departing, destination unknown, south on . . ." Even as he spoke his mind rolled on.

Cas had been assigned to the case two years ago. He'd watched a scared eighteen-year-old girl become a confident twenty-year-old woman in the two years he'd done surveillance. Not for the first time, Cas wishes Jewell had been from a normal family. Not a high-profile political family. That, coupled with lack of evidence, had made an assignment that should have taken several months grow into two years. Budget constraints and discretion had moved the FBI into a desperate situation of using the suspect's own stepsister as bait. It would work if their suspicions about Thad's motivations were correct: Thaddeus MacLeod's long-held blame of Jewell as the star of the family, his jealousy, and need for others to understand and defer to his superiority fueling his rage and desire for retribution against someone he views as the reasons for his perceived failures.

When their intel said it was time to move he'd been equal parts thrilled and terrified at the next part of his job: contact.

And what a contact it had been.

He was supposed to engage the subject, to see if she truly was the missing girl. Cas knew before he started that he was in deep shit. Jewell was wrapped just like he liked them: a shell of fragility layering a core of steel. She was more than beautiful; Jewell was the kind of woman who begged to be taken care of, protected. Cas was supposed to be the one to do that.

Instead, he'd broken every protocol ever constructed, gone against years of training, the rules of engagement and every precept the Bureau possessed. Because of her.

Jewell MacLeod. She'd never been Jess Mackey to him. He'd seen her for the treasure she was. Her real name suited her. He'd nearly fucked up the entire thing at the beginning when he almost called her by her real name.

He'd still fucked up anyway. Cas wouldn't have taken it back for anything. He closed his eyes and remembered her soft body wrapped against his hard one, fitting against his like a glove, her heat engulfing more than his cock; she'd sucked his heart through a straw and drunk him up.

Cas was hers now, she just didn't know it. She couldn't know it just yet. And it hurt. That prick Maverick was a player and something was not quite right with him. Cas had already ordered a background check on him. He looked and moved like a skunk.

Cas was thinking he smelled like shit too.

He was biding his time as Devin Castile. What had begun as necessary dishonesty would soon be revealed. Then maybe they could have something.

If Jewell still wanted him.

He listened to his instructions, nodding slightly, though his superiors couldn't see him agree. "Roger that," he said.

Then he changed frequencies, telling the post at the dorm, "Clearwater, look lively, subject might return." Cas did a quick calculation; it was almost automatic after two years of running numbers and crunching distances. "ETA five minutes."

Cas adjusted his earbud.

White noise greeted him as a response.

"Clearwater?"

Silence; the low buzz of an open mic was the only noise.

*Fuck!*

Cas sprinted for his bike, speaking urgently into the mic, on a frequency that had not been compromised. He flew in a numb fog of self-blame to the university campus.

The other agents moved but it was too late, like it was for Cas. The one nearest the dorm made the gruesome discovery of a ballerina who would dance no more.

When Cas heard about the girl he dropped to his knees, puke rising.

His partner, Agent Luke Adams, found him, and he confirmed it was the other dancer, Shelby Richards, not the subject, Jewell MacLeod.

His Jewell was not dead . . . nor was she safe.

Their ploy to turn the false spotlight on Brock as the killer had drawn Thaddeus MacLeod out like they'd hoped. Now it was time to spring the net. Jewell had always been in danger; but with the death of Amanda Mitchell, the rules of engagement had been changed. Cas had gone from distant surveillance to up close and personal. *So personal.*

Cas shook off the fear for Jewell that threatened to smother him, manning up as he made his way to where forensics were methodically scouring the locker room. When they found the ballet slippers in the dead girl's locker, it was their first break, Jewell's room having yielded nothing of immediate use.

They had been handled by someone other than Jewell or Shelby.

Cas was hoping it was who he thought. They sent the worn slippers to the lab.

Cas could barely let them go, the satin laces running through his gloved fingers as the forensic tech met his eyes, then looked away, bagging them.

He was emotionally compromised and he fucking knew it. Acting like he wasn't would be the biggest challenge of his career. Hell, his fucking life. Adams would watch him closely. Cas straightened his shoulders and started barking orders, commanding all those under him on the investigation.

The background came back on Maverick.

He wasn't Maverick at all, as it turned out. He was a summer-camp acquaintance of Thaddeus MacLeod.

They went way the hell back, over a decade.

Cas's hands became fists, his body shaking in rage. It was his fault. He should have guessed the fuck was somehow connected. But if all they surmised was even half true . . . could it be that they had worked together, killing as many as twelve women, over the space of ten years?

Adams put a hand on his shoulder. "We've got everyone on it, Cas." He looked at Cas with sympathy. "I'm sorry about the girl . . ."

Cas looked at Luke and said, "They killed Clearwater; they've been onto us for a while. That fucker MacLeod, he's a wily sucker."

"And loaded. He's getting funded by Daddy."

"Yeah," Cas said, "isn't this a can of worms."

"The presidential hopeful's psychotic spawn. Fuck. Yeah," Luke said, scrubbing his face.

"And that sick fuck's got Jewell."

They looked at each other, Cas noticing the healing bruises and cuts on Luke's face, which he'd put there, all for show. As the minutes ticked by, they both knew what it meant.

That statistically, it became more likely they'd find a dead Jewell rather than a live Jewell.

Then Cas got the text from the lab and held his cell up in the air in a celebratory gesture.

"People!" he said to the group of agents.

They collectively turned, many faces with hope. A team of twenty had spent two years of their lives trying to save one girl, and all the ones who would come after her. This was their last hope to capture who they believed to be responsible for the deaths of many, to stop deaths in the future. Jewell's unwitting guinea-pig status in the Witness Protection pilot program was the first attempt to dually protect and capture. Now the murderer had the one they were tasked with protecting. They would fail on all counts if he killed who they protected and escaped justice.

Cas hoped he wasn't too late.

The thought of anything happening to Jewell stole the oxygen from his atmosphere.

He forged ahead, telling them where they needed to look.

"We have to hurry; it's an hour if we drive now."

The agents scurried into their respective vehicles.

Cas took his bike; he would arrive before everyone else, even if he had to break every traffic law.

Anything to save Jewell.

## *Two hours prior*

Patrick Boel was ready to speak with Miss Mackey. He had received tentative approval for his prize pupil to audition for the principal role in the next production of the Seattle Pacific Ballet.

*She's more than she seems,* Boel mused, *part enigma.* He had put her through his typical rigorous paces and where other dancers had failed, Miss Mackey had thrived. He could not put his finger on it yet, but she seemed to bloom under the adversity.

That was most excellent, as the ballet was nothing but a series of elite-level dance challenges. Better that she become accustomed to that life now. He would try to convince her to give up college for her true calling.

Jess Mackey had been born to dance; any instructor of dance could see it in her when she began to move. Jess did not simply dance, she *became* the dance.

He knocked tentatively on the girl's locker room door, taking a chance that the dancers might still be there, the halls eerily empty of students.

Patrick Boel had a moment's foreboding flash across the little-used part of his brain most humans ignored.

Had he listened to that precognitive flash, he might have lived to dance another day.

He swung the door inward and saw a huge man fingering what he knew to be Miss Mackey's toe shoes.

Patrick was momentarily stunned to observe two things at once: the man had eyes that were devoid of emotion, and he was also quite certain they seemed familiar to him somehow. It would come to him.

Of course, it never did.

"What are you doing with Miss Mackey's things?" Patrick said, though his heart sped at the gaze that met his, frigid and indifferent.

The large male laid the slipper in the locker with a resigned sigh, giving a subtle signal of some kind to Patrick's right. Mitch will use whatever is at his disposal to get the job done. Between the two of them, Thad is the measured one.

Patrick turned as a dark-haired young man of about six feet two with the palest eyes he had ever seen swung a long tube down in an effort to brain him. Patrick sidestepped easily; after all, he was naturally graceful, strong and fast.

But it was two against one.

Thad grabbed him from behind, Mitch landing the tube deeply in the strong gut of the premier ballet instructor on the West Coast as Thad nearly twisted his head off the stem of his neck.

They collected the slumped and dead form of Patrick Boel.

~

There was no blood and the FBI did not find Boel's body right away. Those lockers hid a myriad of things.

It could have been called sloppy by some, but to their credit, they were trying to save the missing stepdaughter of a South Dakota senator who was even now running for president.

While his unhinged firstborn was in possession of his stepdaughter and suspected in the deaths of twelve women.

Thad had let one clue slip. Boel had interrupted him at precisely the moment when his perfect planning would have prevented such a clue being left.

A fine filament of foliage had dropped from the sleeve of his coat, indigenous to a specific locale, the fabric of his coat having captured it when he was outside, then released it as the temperature and environment changed to the steamy inside of a women's locker room. It had fallen away, landing on the satin slipper, to later be discovered by the forensic team. It stood out from all other trace evidence present.

They knew where that semi-rare plant grew.

Now Cas raced like a black bullet through the night to a summer camp for rich kids. It is there that two mentally deranged teens had come together and begun plotting the deeds that would be discovered by a sheltered and misunderstood Jewell MacLeod. Her friend's death would be the catalyst for her attempt at a brave escape and a life out of the shadow of fear that surrounded her with Thad.

She'd never known about Mitch Maverick.

She did now.

There were no kids at the summer camp in December.

Cas had a feeling there were just three people there now. He hoped to extricate one.

The only one who mattered.

## Jewell MacLeod

I come awake, my mouth dry and swollen from breathing through it, my nose a squished pancake on my face and most likely broken.

I wiggle my fingers and toes, my knee screaming at the small movement, and I bite my lip to stifle the agony. Looking around, I try to find anything that will allow my escape.

Seeing nothing, I feel my old friend defeat try to sink its teeth into me and I shake it off.

I promised Faith at her graveside that I would live, that Thad would be caught, that his brand of evil wouldn't make it into the next generation.

Instead, I'm immobilized on a dirt floor, wheezing through my nose as I gulp desperate air into my lungs, and my knee . . . I feel it with light fingers and it's already swollen, the jeans tight against the joint.

I sit up and my head spins. That's what I get for telling Mitch, or whoever the fuck he was, what I really thought of him.

He hauled off and belted me.

I'm a slow learner; he hit me a second time and knocked me unconscious.

Now my thoughts—those that are the last of my life—turn to Cas.

I wish I was brave enough to tell him what the truth is: *I love him.*

That's all.

That's everything.

A hot tear slides and burns over my wounded face, the tremulous drop of sadness making a perfect circle of grief on the denim covering my broken body.

If I had to do it over again, I wouldn't change my time with Cas. He awoke me from a slumber I didn't know I was in.

I was Sleeping Beauty and Cas was Prince Charming. It's a cliché that I know now is the truth.

My thoughts shatter when I hear male voices, then the one who was La Hunk comes into the narrow doorway, framed for kids, and looks at Thad. "Look who's awake, dancing girl."

He makes me sick.

Thad doesn't say anything. Instead he meets my gaze and smiles.

I'd know that leer anywhere.

I don't think I have the strength to scream but I surprise myself, the birds lifting out of the trees in response to my curdled fear, the sheer terror awakening the things that roam the forest.

They recognize it for what it is and take heed, avoiding the area where a lone woman has come full circle, the predator and the prey together again.

Only one will be victor.

# NINETEEN

~

$\mathscr{M}$itch hauls me off the floor. "Shut your fucking mouth or I'll knock your teeth down your throat . . . *Jewell*."

I shut my mouth, keeping it slightly open to breathe; what little air I get through my beaten nose sounds like a wheezing whistle.

Thad grabs my chin and jerks my face toward his and I flinch. He chuckles. "You did a number on her face."

"You like?" Mitch asks with a thread of manic glee in his voice.

*The bastard.*

Thad slowly nods. "I think I do . . . such delicacy, so easily broken. Like a little china doll."

He drops his hand and flicks a switchblade open. I stifle a whimper, my arms looped through Mitch's and held against his much larger body. It squeezes out of my mouth like the sound of pain it is.

"What are you doing, Thad?" I ask in a low voice, barely more than a whisper, my fear having swallowed its volume.

"I'm afraid Ben here got a little more enthusiastic than slowing you down strictly dictated." Thad smiles.

*Who?*

Thad looks at my face and laughs. "You didn't really think his name was Mitch Maverick, did you?"

Actually, I'm on autopilot; any kind of higher reasoning went out the window when they beat my ballet partner to death and bashed my knee in.

"I chose *Maverick*," Mitch/Ben says next to my ear as I try to tear away from those hands.

He holds me tighter; I can hardly breathe.

"Don't. Bother," he says. "You don't have a chance of escape, Jewell. Neither did Faith."

My breath stops in my throat, arrested in a surreal moment of understanding.

"How do you think I got away with it, Jewell?" Thad asks softly.

I shake my head. *Thad killed Faith.* I heard him do it.

Thad shakes his head ruefully. "You were so sure about everything you found."

Ben says, "It was a team effort and you were getting too nosy."

The pieces came together like shards of jagged glass.

"Where?" I ask.

Thad's eyes narrow and Ben says, "Tell her. We can give her this before we fuck her six ways to Sunday."

My soul groans. I thought it was Thad but it's not just him.

They were working together all this time. And they would do to me what they had done to others.

"I made Ben's fortuitous acquaintance at the camp our parents banished us to each summer." Thad gets a faraway look in his eyes and I watch him remember. "I found a kindred spirit in Ben," he says with a wide grin.

Thad turns away, thunking the blade in a rhythmic pattern against his jeans; my eyes are mesmerized by it. "You should have seen this coming." His pewter eyes meet mine. "You wouldn't quit looking. Every time you found a neighbor's Fido, I would discover your snooping, then threaten you."

"And then your bitch sister told her little friend . . . ," Ben says.

A look of radiance comes over Thad's face. "She was a fighter."

"Yes." Ben breathes his agreement.

I can't help my reaction. The two bastards discussing Faith fighting for her life like a dessert to be savored is too much. I get just enough clearance and drive my elbow into Ben's gut. He makes a satisfying *oof* sound and I stagger away from him.

Thad is on me in seconds, spinning me around on a knee that is no longer flexible and perfect. It stiffly relents, toppling me into him. They've taken everything from me.

"Kill me now, you sick coward," I hiss into his upturned face as I gasp for air from my compromised nose.

"I will, Jewell," he says; his eyes hold the promise of it. "But first, it will be my pleasure to take what you so freely gave that fed."

*What?*

Thad laughs, shaking me until my teeth rattle, Ben moving up beside him. "Who'd you think Devin Castile was?"

*The man I love.*

But I'm struck dumb as more of the misery of my life topples down into puzzle pieces that suddenly fit with sickening clarity.

Transfer student. Looks older than he is. Has mini-vacations where I don't see him and he doesn't communicate.

*Has a secret.*

Thad watches me put it together and slowly nods. "I think Sleeping Beauty has been woken up," Thad tells Ben.

"Well, let's start kissing her then," Ben says.

I see the metal of the switchblade hiss as it zips along the seam of my jeans, tearing a razor-sharp path from hip to ankle.

"No, please . . . ," I beg.

"That swollen knee of yours gets in the way of our fun, Jewell," Ben says with a fake pout.

They cut my jeans off because my knee's too wounded to tear them off.

When I'm standing on one leg in my panties and the thin, shimmering top that seemed so beautiful when I danced with Cas at the club and now lays the barest covering across my body, I begin to plead in earnest.

Thad just shakes his head. "No, Jewell, you're way beyond saving. If you'd just stuck around . . . maybe we could have struck up a bargain."

I shudder. I know what kind of bargain he means.

The corners of his mouth turn down when he sees my expression. "Not too good to spread your legs for Castile."

He grabs my sex like a snake and squeezes me painfully, and I whimper.

Then all hell breaks loose as Ben's head explodes like a watermelon beside me, littering fragments of his sick brain all over me and everything around me.

⌒

Cas watches Thaddeus MacLeod grab his defenseless stepsister in the crotch with vicious intent and sees her face as he hurts her.

A place that Cas has loved with his mouth and the rest of him, tenderly.

His finger depresses the trigger before he consciously decides, the weight of the hammer striking, and a heartbeat later, Benjamin Miller's head pops in a shower of brain matter and blood.

One psychopath down, *one to go.*

Then MacLeod grabs Jewell and uses her as a shield.

⌒

"No!" I yell as gore falls like rain. In a state of shock, I gasp, trying to tear off the shirt that sticks to my skin in a bath of Ben's blood. When Thad takes me against himself, I don't fight, my breaths coming in quick succession, the gorge of my belly rising helplessly inside my chest. I begin to shake and realize shock is overtaking me.

Just as I meet Cas's eyes.

*That might not be his name,* I realize a little randomly, as if from a distance. But there's truth in those eyes and care . . . and a hard edge that, if I looked hard enough, I might have recognized for what it was.

What makes my heart stutter is that Brock stands beside Cas and they come as a team, then Thad has his hand on my throat. The bruising of his fingers will be a necklace of chartreuse thumbprints on my flesh for two weeks afterward.

"I'll break her neck, heroes," Thad says with the ominous certainty of conviction.

My eyes move to Cas's face then my gaze shifts to his bulging biceps. He holds the gun steady on Thad, his thick neck is richly decorated with tattoos that I've traced with my tongue, and a gurgling plea sweeps up inside my throat. I would give all that I am to be with him again.

His eyes flick to mine, then away.

Cas pulls the trigger and a searing pain lances my head.

I feel arms release me and I fall as if in slow motion to the ground.

I am so cold. I lie still as I watch men in black rush around me.

Only one set of eyes I recognize.

Eyes that eat their pupils in ebony totality meet mine; his mouth is moving but no sound is coming out. My ears ring and my body goes numb; something hot and warm slides into my vision. Copper pennies fill my mouth.

Then I'm in his arms. My nose works enough to smell the scents of Cas: mint, musk and male.

I hear his urgent whisper. "Don't you leave me, Jewell."

Then I do.

⌒

The reporters have been camped outside the hospital for a week. Each day I ask the nurse the same question.

*When will they go?*

Her response is always the same: *I don't know.*

It is the story of the decade. I'm the story of the decade. The presidential candidate's stepdaughter discovered, saved by the FBI while his natural son is killed along with an accomplice.

Lone serial killers are rare enough, but a duo?

That I escaped relatively unharmed is being sensationalized across the globe. My eyes move to my knee, hanging suspended by elaborate pulleys. The doctor says I'll have a brace and walk again.

His words stop when I ask if I'll dance.

*He doesn't know.*

Brock was actually Agent Luke Adams and was framed in an elaborate FBI ploy to entice Thad into a false sense of complacency, which worked almost too well. He came out to play, all right, he and . . . Mitch. Who was never who I thought, but a man named Benjamin Miller.

I haven't seen Cas. No surprise there.

The doctors gave me something to dry up my tear ducts. I've cried so much I can't open my eyelids; their angry and swollen slits have begun to interfere with the healing of my nose.

It's almost a good thing, because upon hearing the news that Patrick Boel was murdered and knowing what happened to Shelby, I wept my sadness into the uncaring hospital pillow.

It's a curse to know me. Boel is dead, Shelby too. Just like Faith.

Just when I'm starting to believe my heart is a husk to be blown away on the wind, Carlie bursts through the door.

"Those goddamned butt-sucking leeches!" she yells into the still hospital room. "And that asshat outside the door did an anal probe so I could see you," she whispers in an insulted voice.

Carlie moves toward me and her eyes tell me how bad my face looks.

"Does it hurt?" she asks, and I shake my head.

Carlie's gaze shifts from my healing nose to the leg suspended awkwardly in a sling and sighs.

"I'm so glad it's over, Mackey," she says.

You ever see anyone cry without tears?

Carlie hasn't but knows I'm coming apart and holds me while I sob my dry grief against her.

"Shush, Mackey . . . you're okay. You're okay."

Carlie pulls away.

"I found out that stuff you wanted," she says, handing me a newspaper since the Internet is off-limits for a person just out of the ICU.

I look at the headline:

PRESIDENTIAL CANDIDATE'S STEPDAUGHTER
ESCAPES DEATH AT HANDS OF KILLING BROTHER

"Looks like the old parental unit won't be using the White House as their new 'hood," Carlie says, her eyes on the paper.

I already heard. My stepfather withdrew his bid for the presidency. After all, how could he run for the highest office in America when he couldn't keep his personal house in order?

I set the paper on my lap and Carlie asks, "Can you believe Brock?"

I shake my head.

"He was an agent the whole time." I know that part but it still stings. They used me.

"Must've hurt when Cas beat the shit out of him."

I laugh, then it turns into a cough. Carlie's brows pinch together in concern but I know this lying-on-my-back shit is making me sick. I'm not accustomed to being immobile.

"Brock—I mean, Agent Adams—sure made it real enough . . . are the FBI allowed to hit the people they protect?" she asks, and I shrug. "I'd love to be a fly on you-know-who's hot ass after he belted you. Authenticity much?" Carlie asks in a whisper, "Have you seen him?"

I don't meet her eyes. "I dream of him," I say just as quietly.

"I'm sure there's a reason he hasn't come to see you. I mean, Mackey"—she looks into my eyes, the roots of my hair grown out in a narrow copper stripe at the crown of my head—"he saved you. He came . . . he—"

"Don't say it, Carlie." I can't stand the sympathy. I'm lucky to be alive when so many around me are not. That's what the media should be doing, celebrating their lives instead of focusing on an insecure woman.

"I have to, Mackey."

I cross my arms and she ignores me.

"He couldn't tell you he was FBI; they'd tracked Thad to the school. He'd have blown his cover if he told you the truth."

I glare at her, though it isn't Carlie I'm mad at.

"So fucking me against walls was part of his job description?" I ask.

She shrugs helplessly. "All I know is he's feelin' you, girlfriend. He was doing a job and still wanted to be with you, y'know?"

I don't know. I don't want to know. Cas lied. That's it.

*He also saved me.*

His existence awoke my own.

"Think about it, Mackey. Don't throw something away that could be amazing because you don't understand it."

I cast my eyes down at the printed hospital sheet, turning her words over in my mind.

Carlie stands, the awkwardness a barrier between us. I'm distant for other reasons now. They have nothing to do with her.

She leans close and kisses my cool cheek. "I love you, dancer."

I stare at her without tears. "I love you too."

Carlie walks out and that night I fall into fitful sleep. I dream of Cas, that he comes to me and tells me the truth. Who he is . . . *that he loves me.*

I know it's only a dream.

## Cas

Cas watches Jewell sleep from the FBI guard station and she never knows. Just as she hasn't for almost two weeks.

The doctor approaches. "Agent Steel, why don't you visit her when she is awake?" he asks.

*Because I can't.* "How is she?" Cas evades the question with one of his own.

The doctor sighs. "She's improving but is vulnerable to infection. Because she was in such good physical condition, we will put her leg in the brace tomorrow . . ."

"Her face?" Cas turns and the doctor takes a step back from the aggression he sees there.

"She won't be disfigured, if that's what you're asking, but she's going to look pretty beat up for a while," he answers with simple honesty.

Cas nods. But before he walks away he says, "Don't tell her—"

"You were here," the doctor says, finishing for him. "You've made that abundantly clear, Agent Steel."

Cas gives a grim smile, then walks away.

The doctor knows she'll never remember but Agent Steel brought her in. It was Agent Blaine "Cas" Steel who stayed by her side until she was stabilized. It took ten hours. She'd lost blood from the grazing head wound she'd received, and shock had worsened her condition.

Yet, the young agent stayed, his hard eyes scanning each face that got near the young dancer until he had cataloged them all.

The doctor enters Jewell's room, watching her toss and turn in the bed. He thinks he hears a word.

*Cas.*

He shrugs; it could be an old man's wishful thinking.

## Life

I'm so ready.

Carlie is here to pick me up and there isn't a dry eye on the ward where I've been imprisoned. Excuse me, I mean . . . *recovering*.

I have a soft cast on and a recurring appointment with a physical therapist. The horrible bruises are gone from underneath my eyes and I can breathe again.

My parents have paid for the plastic surgeon who made my lightning strike of a scar look like a thin whip of nothing on my smooth forehead.

A stylist came to the hospital and dyed my hair to its natural color.

I'm Jewell MacLeod again; I've always been her.

When I walk out into the blinding strobes of the reporters' cameras I frantically search for Carlie, the nurse's steady hand a band of comfort on my thin arm, the crutch helping my bad side as I hobble along.

"Miss MacLeod!" a reporter exclaims, and I flinch away from a microphone crammed almost under my nose.

"Tell us about your miraculous rescue!"

There are shouted questions from all corners and all of them are ground glass on my nerves.

Then, as if I'm in a desert and seeing a mirage, Cas is there, like he was that day at the audition.

My eyes narrow down to pinpoints on his large body as it leans against a nondescript black SUV, with dark leather and sunglasses to match. The cool January weather is a pewter backdrop to his inky form, his muscular arms folded across his chest. He stands and with a loose, graceful gait, he strides with purpose.

And he is coming toward me.

One of the sharper reporters catches my shell-shocked look and they turn en masse to see a six-foot-four moving black wall of muscled male coming for the survivor of a serial-killer team that he wiped out like the blight on society they were. A bullet for each sick mind.

They part and watch him come down the middle of their stunned group. A lone cameraman recovers and lets his camera roll.

The nurse lifts her hand from my arm and steps away with my crutch in her hand, hanging at my elbow in case I need her, as Cas moves within inches of me and I tilt my head up to meet his eyes.

Deep ebony meets green as I hold my emotions together by the thinnest thread.

"Agent Steel! Agent Steel!" a tenacious woman reporter blares from beside us. "Tell us what plan the FBI has for Miss MacLeod."

"I don't know," Cas says so quietly I can almost feel them lean forward to capture his words. Cas's hand brushes my cheek, and I close my eyes and move my face into that warm caress as the heat from the cameras flash behind my closed lids.

Then both hands cradle my face and my eyes open.

He looks at me for a moment that is both savagely long and too brief. "My plan is to love her," he says to me and me alone.

I stand up on tiptoe, my leg encased in its cast dangling, and Cas scoops me up by my waist with one arm while the other holds my head as he presses me to his lips and the cameras flash and burn.

Our love etched forever for the world to see.

# TWENTY

~

*One year later*

I watch his forearm muscles ripple as Cas puts the finishing touches on the spare room. It's a narcissistic mess of floor-to-ceiling mirrors with metal barres bisecting all that smooth glass.

He steps away from tightening the last screw, the last lick of paint on the ceiling still tacky, the inset surround-sound speakers unobtrusively tucked in the corners of the ceiling and nearly invisible, so closely do they match the surrounding paint color.

I walk smoothly to him in the center of the wood floor, moving into first position. I slowly rise on my toes and he captures me around my waist, jerking me to him hard, pecking my face everywhere with petal-soft kisses that promise harder ones to come.

"You like it?" he asks between hard pants and harder kisses.

"I do, Agent Steel," I say, my arms twined around his neck. "Only one week until I begin at SPB—"

"I'm so proud of you, Jewell," Cas says, interrupting me in a low voice, planting a sweet kiss on my open mouth, cinching me tighter against himself.

"Stop doing it standing up, you sluts," Carlie says casually as she waltzes inside the newly refurbished dance studio. "Wow," she breathes, "this is so completely the bomb. Just sayin'."

*I think so too.* "Yes, it is." I smile at Cas and he turns to Carlie. "Timing sucks as usual, Carlie."

She puckers her face and sticks out a tongue. "So deal, don't you have a murderer or someone to catch?"

He sighs. "Always," he says, pushing a hand through hair that's grown out . . . to about an inch. *Just enough to grip,* I think with a small smile.

He leans down, grabbing the back of the knot of my hair and pulling my face against his. Kissing me thoroughly, he says against my mouth, "You okay, babe?"

I nod.

He looks over at Carlie. "I'll be back."

"Yeah, pal . . . like the Terminator."

He scowls and she grins. "Just go, Cas . . ." I laugh and he does, swatting my ass as he leaves. Of course, that makes me want him to stay. Badly. I feel it all the way to my toes . . . and other places.

"Gawd, girl, you got it bad."

I look at Carlie, who's all smiles. "Yeah, I do."

"I don't know why." She rolls her eyes.

When the silence comes I know what she's here for. She doesn't pull punches. "So tomorrow's a year," she says, meeting my eyes.

"Yeah."

"You gonna do it?"

I nod. "Yes."

"It can't be easy . . . ," she says with sympathy.

I lace my hands together and blow my hair up and away from my eyes. When I look at her I tell the truth. "It's bigger than me. Shelby died. Instructor Boel . . . and all those girls . . ." I clasp my hands tighter, the knuckles whitening with just the thought of speaking at the memorial.

"For Faith," I say. Somehow, the pain of the last three years without Faith has come full circle. It no longer bites at the edges of me. Thad is gone. Cas and I are together . . . like Faith would want. She's gone, but not forgotten.

Carlie smiles at me and I smile back. "For Faith," she repeats. When she hugs me I cry real tears, wet ones.

They won't be my last but they are no longer as sad.

I wear black and look for a friendly face in the sea of faces that stare at me. My eyes hit on Carlie and Amber and my shoulders relax. The tension I didn't realize was there eases further when a large, strong palm warms the small of my back.

I clear my throat and begin to speak, the flowers bright dots against a black backdrop of mourners' clothes.

"A year ago today, I was in hiding . . . and by being in hiding, I helped no one. The following people impacted my life and died because of their association with me."

I bite my lip for a moment and Cas squeezes my hip, his solid, warm presence behind me affirming me, uplifting me.

I continue. "Though I no longer blame myself for the choices of two very disturbed people, I want to acknowledge that I am who I am today because of Patrick Boel and my fellow dancer Shelby Richards." I choke back my tears but they break through my voice like a horse at the starting gate. "They believed in me without knowing who I truly was. And for that, I will always be grateful . . ."

People stand. They add their flowers to the others until there is a mountain of fragrance and color covering the memorial. A rainbow of hope.

When my last word echoes into the silence, I allow Cas to half carry me to our car.

The reporters wait like vultures, their eyes trained on the ring finger of my left hand. They miss nothing.

But Brock is there. Actually, I've almost got myself trained into thinking of him by his proper name, Luke Adams, partner to my future husband, Blaine "Cas" Steel.

He'll always be Cas to me.

That's the one thing he's always given me.

His name. Now I'll have both, that one piece of truth and his name to share.

Luke blocks the reporters' view of us as we slide into the SUV, secure behind the black tinted windows, and slam the door after he sweeps inside the rig.

I lay my head on Cas's shoulder and he presses a kiss against my temple. "I'm proud of you, babe."

I turn my face to his, tears held tightly inside my eyes; I

keep them wide so they won't fall. I've cried enough. "You think?" I ask.

"I do." Then he kisses me like his partner isn't in the front seat and twenty reporters aren't circling the vehicle like sharks.

That's how Cas always kisses me.

# ACKNOWLEDGMENTS

*You*, my reader.

*My husband*, who is my biggest fan.

*Erica Spellman-Silverman* and the Trident Media Group team
for giving me a chance.

*Lauren*, for believing in my work.

*Alex*, for improving my work; it sounds better because of you.

*Aja Pollock*, my copy editor.

*Beth*, a big supporter of my work, and of me as well; priceless.

*My Aussie Girl*, I love ya.

*Di*, who has a case of Reviewer's Ass, I've been told . . . you
keep me sane.

*Crystal* (who was somehow the loveable and witty Carlie)

*Rônin*, my warrior